To Di

Thanks for
your comments.

Sue Venable

DWELLING AMONG THE UNTRODDEN WAYS

Life in Oklahoma Territory

by

Sue Livesay Venable

ISBN-13: 978-0692968000
ISBN-10: 0692968008

ACKNOWLEDGMENTS

My interest in Oklahoma history came from the tales of pioneers who settled in Oklahoma Territory. My paternal grandparents, Anderson and Laura Livesay, made this same trip from Schell City, Missouri, to Pawnee County, Oklahoma Territory, accompanied by their five children, Nelle, Opal, Donna, Daisy, and Owen.

However, by the time I became interested in writing about their adventures, they were deceased. There were so many times I wished I could ask them about what route they took, how they found their way without roads, and how they stayed alive over such a long journey. So I had to read the diaries of other settlers through the marvelous Oklahoma Historical Society archives. The Mansfield family's adventures are mostly from my imagination, even though they are based on the historical facts of Pawnee County.

I am indebted to many people for their help in my research and writing. Bruce Peverley, Agriculture Extension Educator for Oklahoma State University, shared his knowledge of agriculture in Pawnee County, and Darole Mott provided his experiences on his farm in northwest Oklahoma. Their conversations gave me a basic plan for the farmer's calendar of planting. Royse Parr, Tulsa attorney and geology authority and author, explained the history of the Red Bed Plains of Pawnee County. Special thanks must go to Kenneth V. Bloom, a fine author, for his help with formatting. John Wooley and Dr. Linda Reese, both established Oklahoma authors, provided excellent suggestions after very careful reading of my book. Chelsea Vaughn Showalter shared her wisdom of the publishing business. Judy Mott, my dear friend and fellow English teacher at Monte Cassino School, provided insight and expertise on details of the rough draft.

Most of all, I am thankful to my family through the past decade. My daughters, Cathy and Amy, were enthusiastic readers whose creative minds kept me striving to write more. My husband, Brice, showed patience and understanding for my solitary writing times.

Lastly, my 38 years as a teacher gave me the desire to write a book on Oklahoma history that would attract young readers. I was determined to create a story that they would find appealing as they learned about the early days of our amazing state.

Anderson and Laura Livesay are pictured here on their wedding day, January 19, 1888, in Flat Rock, Vernon County, Missouri. They were the author's inspiration for the fictional Mansfield family who appear in this book.

CHAPTER ONE

Johnson grass opened up for the awkward covered wagon as it plowed a furrow that would never hold seed. Early April in southern Missouri with its promise of new life had always filled Laura with such joy. But now she wondered what lay ahead. Anderson had predicted a pleasant, comfortable journey down into Oklahoma Territory in the beauty of springtime, but already the geography did not match her dreams. All she saw was stubble, bothersome foxtails, and ugly trees projecting their gnarled arms against an indifferent sky.

As a late afternoon sun tried to tan her thin arms, the girl-woman looked longingly at the murky horizon. The grandmotherly bun that organized her light-auburn hair seemed out of place on a head that possessed such a dewy complexion and tender eyes. Yet, her clenched fists were the hands of a man, muscular and rough, revealing a toilsome past.

She glanced at Anderson sitting beside her, driving the team that transported all their worldly goods, their five sleeping children, and a small dog. This rigid farmer struck a sharp contrast to the seventeen-year-old boy who claimed her as his bride back in Missouri a dozen years before. "Mr. Look Down" was her nickname for him because of his habit of staring at his feet whenever anyone passed. Yet, his shyness had attracted her. Every Tuesday when he delivered eggs to the orphanage, Laura maneuvered her way to the kitchen door just to see him. Since she had lived there since childhood, the matron would let her pick her chores. One Tuesday at the back door, Laura had made an impression because the next Wednesday night he sat with her at Baptist prayer meeting. After a year of courtship, their marriage followed in the spring.

The shyness that attracted her then had now changed to passivity, as he took the buffets of life without reaction. Early on in their marriage, she learned to conceal her feelings. She told herself that his unfeeling nature might just be a sign of strength. Though she was thankful for that strength, many times she had yearned for his understanding.

"Don't cry anymore" was his response to the loss of their firstborn. "Poor hapless babe," she had murmured as they placed him in an unmarked grave. But she knew her tears must be inner ones to match the resolute nature of the dry-eyed man who completed the simple burial. The six-month-old baby had lost his life in a typhoid epidemic.

Laura never knew her own parents. The orphanage was her earliest memory of home, and the rumors of a large family that had to give her away at birth were her only shreds of ancestry. She had longed for the day when she as a mother would supply the missing link for her own child. Now the equation echoed in her mind: the parentless child equals the childless parent. Anderson wouldn't even let her name the baby.

"Why waste a good name? We might need that name later on." Secretly she christened him Esau, knowing his birthright had been lost.

One year later a baby girl was born to them. They named her Nelle. They had hoped for a boy and had named the unborn baby Eugene as farmers needed sons to help with the heavier farm work. So Eugene became Nelle Eugene, and she learned to work beside her father. Then came Opal, Donna, Daisy and Owen. Five children, and the fifth was a son. Anderson had prayed daily for the last one.

Now all five were asleep in the moving wagon. At the birth of each child, Laura was haunted by the responsibility of motherhood. Until this moment she at least felt secure in knowing about life in Missouri. Now she thought of the five innocents traveling to an unknown land. Were they hostages with an unknown destiny?

Yet, Laura tried to believe that their lives were changing for the better. From Schell City, Vernon County, Missouri, they were traveling to their new home on land that Anderson had earned through the Cherokee Strip Land Run back in 1893. He had tried for a homestead and filed a claim on 160 acres. There was talk that this Oklahoma Territory would be a state some day soon.

Laura remembered his aloofness as she quizzed him about details of the day. What were his thoughts as he waited for the starting gun? How many men brought their wives to watch? What was their new land like? To all of these questions he had given numbed responses. Now the prairie schooner, swaying on its moorings, heightened the vague uneasiness that fluttered inside her. She looked for a road that never appeared. Suddenly yanking the reins, Anderson brought the team to a halt. "Laura, I have to tell the truth about this trip. I lied to you, but just hear me out."

Stunned and frightened, Laura listened as the tale unfolded.

"Here it is. At the start of the run, everything was fine. I had my eye on a great spot of bottom land down by a creek. Jake was a new horse to me, but he showed a good spirit. I knew he could handle the strain and the excitement, and you know what a good rider I am."

She nodded slowly, still puzzled, but strangely relieved that at least he was eager to talk about the mysterious run.

"The September sun was beating down on us. With a good breeze at our back, I felt sure this was going to be my lucky day. I can't explain the excitement and noise with 100,000 people lined up for the land and even more when you added up the onlookers. Then, at high noon, the guns sounded, and Jake took the noise in stride as he darted out, finding a path through that mob. We were heading out, ahead of most of those jaspers, when all of a sudden Jake stumbled and fell. He just fell and couldn't rise. My heart sank. I was thrown to the ground and was staring at a blamed prairie dog hole. Laura, that cursed rodent had ruined our hopes. Folks were yelling at me to—I won't tell you what they yelled. Poor Jake was in such pain with his leg broken that I had to shoot him right there."

Laura had listened to the whole shocking story. Then she pleaded, "Tell me that we aren't going out there to be beggars!"

"No, Laura," he continued. "We'll have a place, thanks to the Pawnee Indians. You know those letters

4

I've been getting lately. Well, I've made a deal with one of those Pawnees to use part of his allotment. Each one was given 160 acres, and most of them aren't interested in farming. We'll be sharecroppers for a few years, but we do have a place to live."

"Then why didn't you just tell me the truth?" asked Laura. "You couldn't help it that Jake tripped. I would have understood."

Right then Laura saw a side of her husband that had been hidden all the time. After a pause, Anderson said slowly, "I just couldn't tell the awful story. I was afraid you wouldn't come with me. We'll get there in time to plant some corn. And we'll follow with some winter wheat. You'll see. Then next spring we'll have a real crop."

As she looked across the horizon at the fading sunset, Laura knew she should offer some words of encouragement, but she found no words. He had been hiding the awful truth from her for five years. All she could do was pull her blue sunbonnet down over her eyes to hide the tears.

CHAPTER TWO

All night Laura fought her feelings of despair as she looked at her family asleep in the wagon. She knew she must come to terms with her fears before morning broke. The resentment over Anderson's betrayal was gnawing at her, and her prayers were that God would show her how to forgive.

At daybreak she knew she must ready herself for a new attitude. As she climbed down from the wagon to start the fire for breakfast, she took a deep breath to calm her nerves. Within minutes she had coffee ready and was preparing eggs and biscuits. Anderson surprised her as he walked softly toward the fire and took her hand. Although he was relieved that he had finally revealed the truth about his misadventure in the land run, he was still unsure about her acceptance of their new situation. He hesitated to speak and waited for her to open the conversation. She offered him his mug of hot coffee. The children were still asleep, and she captured their few moments together to let him know she was at peace with him.

"I've been wondering about what kind of house we will have out there in Pawnee County," she said.

Encouraged by the kindness in her voice, Anderson slowly began to describe the possibilities for a shelter.

"Well, at first we'll just be camping out in the wagon. We should be pretty skilled at that by then. As soon as we can, we'll start building one of those dugouts. I've heard they are pretty cozy and can be big enough for the time being."

As Laura heard the word "dugout," she shivered at the thought of living in the ground. Anderson saw her quivering so hard that her coffee was spilling onto the ground.

"It's not as bad as you might think," he assured her. "Just remember. It's temporary. All the time we are living that way, I'll be building us a nice log cabin. Keep your mind on that picture. By next spring, we'll be clean and warm in our own cabin. That land we're renting has plenty of post oaks, and the Indian has promised me that we can use them for building our home. Then we'll turn the dugout into shelter for the livestock."

Laura asked about the dirt floor and dirt walls. Anderson assured her that a rug could go on the dirt floor and newspaper could cover the walls. He estimated a 24' by 12' room with tree trunk supports and a quilt hung for privacy would work for the family. He planned to make the dwelling high enough for his six-foot body to be able to walk without stooping. "Just think of the first year as a great adventure. Our children will have stories to tell for the rest of their lives." He neglected to tell her the stories he had heard about the territorial settlers having to use sand for soap and children spending afternoons collecting cow chips for fuel since coal was so expensive. Just then, the children were waking up and ready for their breakfast.

With the rising sun, what had appeared to be a deserted countryside began to teem with life. Cardinals

7

were singing in a nearby mulberry tree, and the Mansfield children added their playful voices.

Laura knew that Nelle and Opal would organize the younger ones. By the time the five children found their way to the campfire, a hearty breakfast awaited them. Donna and Daisy brought little Owen to the camp blanket that Nelle and Opal had carefully laid on the ground.

"Mama, can I stir the eggs this morning?" asked Opal. "Nelle got to do it yesterday."

"All right, if you are extra careful near the fire."

Opal smiled at the thought of a new task, but she also was relieved that Nelle would be left with the tending of three-year-old Owen. He was a dear little brother but could be a real chore to keep safe.

Back at the wagon, Anderson was readying the two horses for the day's journey and checking the condition of their hooves. Today he hoped to cover more territory, and the key to the success of this trip lay in the horses' well-being. His disaster at the Cherokee Strip Run had taught him that fact.

Joining him at the wagon, Laura asked, "How are Blaze and Belle doing? Are they ready to take us down the road today?"

"I feel good about them," said Anderson. "There aren't any abrasions on their legs, and the horseshoes look good. My only fear is that pulling seven of us is going to cause some cartilage damage to those horses eventually."

Laura knew what that fear meant: they had to save these horses from harm. She remembered other travelers' stories about walking behind the wagon. Bravely she responded, "I am ready to walk from time to time."

"You're a good woman," said Anderson. "This next stretch may need that brave attitude, especially when we reach the hills near Lamar. The horses will have enough stress just pulling the wagon on an uphill grade."

Laura knew the children must be prepared for this likely possibility. Her challenge was to make the walking less of a chore and more of a game. Returning to the campfire, she discovered that Nelle and Opal had extinguished the fire, drenching the coals with water from a nearby stream. She continued the cleanup and organized the children back into the wagon.

Anderson was ready for the day's journey as he called out, "All aboard? This train is leaving the station!"

Donna, sitting behind her mother, asked, "Why does he like to pretend we are on a train?"

Laura thought a minute and said, "Probably because he wishes this were a train. Or maybe it's because he is remembering the train ride he took down to the Cherokee Strip Run."

In her childhood innocence, Donna asked, "Papa, tell us about your train ride and all about the Cherokee Strip Run!"

Anderson breathed deeply, checked to see that everyone was safely tucked in for the morning ride, and prepared for a long story.

CHAPTER THREE

Clearing his throat, Anderson looked across at Laura who gave him a nod of approval. "Well, seeing as it's a long day on our trip into Lamar, I have plenty of time to tell you about that journey to the Cherokee Strip Run."

"First of all, I heard about the run from some fellows back at Schell City. They were excited about free land down in the territory and talked me into joining them in this big giveaway. I couldn't see that I had anything to lose, so your mama and I agreed I should try to stake a claim."

"To get there, we guys rode a train. I hope you all can go on one of those sometime. You just sit there and watch the land whiz by. Once we got to the starting place, it was like nothing I'd ever seen. People had come from all around. Some were dignified-looking men in fine clothing. Others looked like they might have just served time and probably had. For two days it was hard to find a place to sleep or eat, but we knew why we had come and made the best of it."

"Some families were there all planning to make the run in a covered wagon. I saw men on bicycles; some even tried to run on foot. But the best deal seemed to be making the run on horseback. Of course, I didn't have a horse, so I had to find one."

"This was the time for shysters and the get-rich-quick guys, so horses were not cheap. I walked all over for six hours the day before to find a horse that was cheap enough and capable of making the run. Finally, about sunset the night before the race I found an honest-looking man who offered me a horse named Jake. By that time, I guess I was easy to please, but that Jake had a good feel to him. I had to pay fifty dollars, but I had to have a horse."

"Well, that night I slept in the horse stall at the livery stable with Jake, just so no one would steal him. The next morning, he and I had a good breakfast and made our way through the crowd. There were U.S. cavalrymen all along the starting line. Behind them were all the people waiting for the signal."

"How many people were in the run?" asked Nelle.

"You won't believe this, but there were 100,000 people trying to stake a claim on that land. And the sad thing was that there was not enough land for even half of those people."

"Oh, Papa. I feel sorry for the people who lost out," sighed Opal. "Imagine how those people felt."

"Yes. Well, not everyone wins," continued Anderson, temporarily losing his desire to finish the tale. He gazed at the horses until Nelle brought him back to the story.

"Then what happened?" she begged.

"Oh, yes. I promised you a story," he said. "Well, at noon on September 16, the sun was hotter than I can ever remember. The wind had picked up in the night, and dust was blowing so hard that you could hardly see. The crowd got quiet waiting for the signal. Then it came as the cavalrymen blew their bugles, and we all set forth."

"Did you win the race, Papa?" asked Donna.

"Well, you'll see. Just let me tell you in my own way."

Daisy said, "I hope no dogs got hurt. I just hate it when someone is mean to a dog." She hugged the little beagle close to her side.

Laura patted her and told her not to interrupt.

Anderson knew he had to get to his personal tragedy. "The fast horses led the way, followed by the wagons, and then there were the accidents. I was back behind two covered wagons, one with a family inside and the other driven by one man. The family sped out in front and caused the other wagon to turn over. They kept on going even though the man was out of the race with a wounded horse. You see, it was very dangerous to stop or even slow down with all those people forcing you ahead. I managed to steer Jake out of the way and continued the race for about a mile. I saw some people driving stakes into their claims and others just giving up. As I sped on, I had to steer clear of several fights that broke out along the way."

Laura sensed that her husband was stalling with detail to keep from getting to the major event of his story. She moved closer and gently squeezed his rough hand.

Donna smiled at the exciting turn of her father's story. "Then what happened?"

"Well, this is how it went. Just as I began to think my chances were good in reaching the good land I had been hoping for, I felt Jake go down. Suddenly we were both in the dirt with horses pounding their feet beside us. The dust was blinding me. Remember this. I'm pretty doggoned lucky to be alive to tell you this story. How I kept from being killed I'll never know. I managed to jump out of the way of some other riders and looked back at Jake. He was lying there with a broken leg."

"No, Papa. What happened?" cried Nelle.

"Well, you see, there was a prairie dog hole, and he had tripped in it. He broke his leg. I had to shoot him."

"No. You didn't shoot a horse, did you, Papa?" cried Opal.

"Yes. I know it sounds cruel, but it had to be," answered Anderson.

Donna sobbed, "Oh, Papa, would you shoot Blaze and Belle?"

By now, all five children were crying, and Laura drew them close to her, saying, "Of course he wouldn't. Your papa had no other choice. The poor horse was in such pain and couldn't ever recover."

After a brief time, Nelle asked, "Papa, does this mean you were one of the losers in the run?"

Anderson swallowed hard and admitted, "You could say that, I guess. I didn't stake a homestead, but I have land promised for us to work. Don't worry. We'll have a new home in Oklahoma Territory. Our farm is waiting for us in Pawnee County."

He told just enough to calm the children. The words "home" and "farm" gave them hope of better days. Opal was still in tears over the dead horse, but she didn't get upset about the free 160 acres being lost. Donna, Daisy and Owen were feeling drowsy by this time after such a long story and snuggled in the bedding of the wagon. Only Nelle pondered what kind of farm and work awaited her family if it belonged to someone else.

CHAPTER FOUR

The quiet morning ride was an easy one with large cottonwoods providing dense shade. However, as the shadows grew shorter and the sun came to be directly overhead, the former flat trail began to rise, foretelling the hill country Anderson had predicted.

"Laura, we'll have to help Belle and Blaze in a few miles. This uphill grade is not fair to them," he said.

Laura volunteered to walk, but Anderson had a better plan. He explained, "Since I am the heaviest, and we need an adult to handle two horses, you need to drive. I'll carry Daisy, and Nelle can carry Owen. Opal and Donna can trade off riding and walking."

Laura agreed and then explained the procedure to the children, trying to make the piggyback plan sound like a game. Instead, the children suggested other plans. Nelle offered to drive the horses; Opal and Donna wanted to be full-time walkers. Even Owen cried over being the one who was carried.

Anderson pulled the reins for an unexpected stop. "Now you children stop that. I know you mean well, but you listen to us. We know best." The stern tone alerted them to follow his rules, and all five children fell into line.

The first mile was the easy part. Owen and Daisy, being the youngest ones, rode piggyback and chuckled most of the way. Papa carried his load without any struggle, but Nelle was suffering under the strain of her little brother. The next two sisters, Opal and Donna, were able to endure their walk-then-ride plan. By the end of the first mile, Mama had a new idea.

She drew the horses to a stop and called out to her husband, "This is a straight trail, and the horses are not needing much guidance. Why don't we let Nelle drive, and I'll carry Owen?"

Nelle was thrilled at the prospect of riding and guiding those two gentle horses. She shouted, "I'm ready for the challenge!"

As she climbed aboard and took over the reins, Laura warned her that a firm grip was necessary. "The horses will sense your fear through your hands. You speak to the horses through the reins, and that message is stronger than words. Don't do any sudden jerking or yelling. You've watched your papa do this. Just pretend you are Papa. And it helps to sing softly to them. Belle really likes that. And don't forget about the brake lever when you need to stop the wagon. It connects with the rear wheel. Can you remember all those things?"

Nelle was so excited that she forgot to be nervous. It had all looked so easy.

"I'll be fine. I'm going to pretend I am Papa."

When Laura joined Anderson as a walker, he whispered, "Do you really think Nelle can do this? Can a nine-year-old handle those two horses?"

Laura knew that confidence was key to success for Nelle. "Don't let her hear you. I have seen her churn butter and lift heavy boxes for two years. She has a way with those two horses, and they trust her. Let's trust her to take the wagon along this slight hill for the next mile."

As she carried Owen safely behind the wagon, Laura was praying that Nelle's young arms would convey that confidence to the two friendly beasts leading the way. Then she heard the girlish voice singing "Camp town Races" and knew everything would be all right. "Bet my money on a bob-tailed nag. Somebody bet on the bay."

Nelle continued her concert through two more songs from Stephen Foster and was just starting "Jeanie with the Light Brown Hair" when Anderson called out to her, "Rein them in, Nelle. Brake lever. Time to stop." The trail was flattening out and not a minute too soon.

As she dropped the reins, Nelle felt her hands shaking from the strain. She was ready to be a child again and leave the hard work to adults. Her papa gave her a hug and thanked her for a job well done. Quickly she joined her siblings in the wagon for a restful journey in the late afternoon.

CHAPTER FIVE

After traveling for five days, the family had covered seventy miles. Soon they would leave their home state and enter the Twin Territories. Driving the covered wagon into Joplin, Missouri, Anderson told Laura the plans for the night.

"We'll find a city park here where travelers are welcome to hitch a wagon overnight. It should be close to the livery stable, according to this map that Sam Jeeter drew. I'll sleep here in the wagon to protect our things. Laura, you and the children can find a room at the inn on the main street. It's just a block away from the park. I'll give you enough cash for a good night's sleep. Heaven knows you all need it."

Laura interrupted with "How can we be sure we will ever see you again? I have a sinking feeling that we should stay together."

"Nonsense. Now just remember to keep the money in your shoe at all times. Don't let anyone see it. All we can afford is one bed, but that sure beats the last five nights spent in the wagon."

Anderson watched carefully as his family slowly moved toward the inn. Close by, he noticed a gathering of covered wagons in a field near the creek. It looked like the wayside park on the map. Finding an empty spot, he drew the horses to a stop, then patted the spotted horse, talking to it as to an old friend. "Here we are, Blaze. All we own is back there in the schooner. You let me know if you smell danger." Checking the wagon, he sensed it was a good time to use the grease bucket hanging from the axle to coat the wheels.

Just then, one of the other travelers appeared. Short and sinewy, he walked with an impressive confidence.

"Howdy. Looks like you are heading west to a new life like the rest of us. My name's Roscoe Gaines."

Although Anderson usually distrusted strangers, there was something in this man's face that set him at ease. "Why, yes, we are on our way to Oklahoma Territory," he answered.

Roscoe slapped his dusty knee and gave a hearty laugh. "Well, I'll be darned if you ain't the second guy tonight who told me that! See that wagon over yonder under those scrub oaks? He's headin' out to Pawnee. Ain't that in Oklahoma Territory?"

Still not wanting to tell everything, Anderson nodded. "Yes, I might want to meet that guy."

Roscoe, sensing that his new acquaintance wouldn't make the first move, whistled between his teeth, and shouted, "Hey, Frank, get over here!"

Soon a tall, lanky fellow in well-worn overalls ambled up to the wagon and extended a rough hand. "Howdy do."

Roscoe explained, "Frank, you should meet this guy because you're both headin' to Oklahoma Territory. Maybe you could compare notes."

Anderson got down off the wagon. "My name is Anderson Mansfield, and we might be following the same trail."

Frank quickly added, "Just to keep on track, I'll give you my last name, too. It's Barnes. In fact, that's the whole Barnes family over there bedded down for the night. Why don't you join us at our campfire and rest for a spell?"

As Anderson sat down on a rumpled quilt, he began to feel his way carefully into a new relationship. "Roscoe here tells me that you are on your way to Pawnee. How did you choose that faraway place?"

Then Frank gave his tale. "Well, I tell you. Back in 1893 I was part of the Cherokee Strip Run. I guess you've heard of that one since it was the largest land run. I had high hopes of claiming my 160 acres and living there for five years to become a landowner, but I lost out. What I thought was open land had already been claimed by another guy. We fought over it at the land office, but I didn't stand a chance."

At this point, Anderson wanted to tell his own story, but his old shyness held him back.

Frank continued the saga. "So, you'll never know how hopeless I felt. Hopeless and sad. Sad, nothing! I was mad enough to fight. But the other fella had the law on his side. Of course, I know it could have been lots worse. Why, there were some guys who even ended up with a dead horse in all that commotion. Can you imagine how they felt! Well, I guess you really had to be there."

All that Anderson could do was stare at his dusty boots. Then he asked, "So, what is the point in going out west if you lost the land?"

"Well, sir. Here's the beautiful part. You probably heard about those Pawnee Indians getting an allotment of 160 acres each in what is now Pawnee County. They had lived in eastern Nebraska, but around 1870 to 1880

they were forced to move down into Oklahoma
Territory. Then when each Indian got his allotment, the
old style of life had changed. Gone were their buffalo
hunts on the prairie. They were forced into farming,
and they hated it. You can't blame them for that. So,
lucky for me, I found a Pawnee Indian who is renting
his land to me."

The parallel story forced Anderson to break his
silence. "I'm doing the same thing—renting from an
Indian." There was no reason to tell about his own
disappointment in the same famous race or the prairie
dog hole or the loss of the horse.

"Well, I'll be darned! And where is this rental land?"
asked Frank.

Without a pause, Anderson said, "It's in Pawnee
County, Oklahoma Territory. We could be neighbors."

Frank let loose with a shout that woke the drowsing
Roscoe.

"What's goin' on? Did I miss something?"

"I guess you did, my friend," said Frank. "This fella
here just might be my farming buddy. He's heading
out to Pawnee, too!"

"Well, sir, I'm mighty proud for both of you. If I
were a youngun like you guys, I'd set out for the new
land myself. But my wife has folks in Miami, over in
Indian Territory, and we're fixin' to join her brother in
runnin' a general store. That's about as darin' as I can
be."

"Yeah, you're so right," answered Frank. "But we're
all gambling our lives on a new land. Why, we can't
even say we're going to a new state; it's just called the
Twin Territories."

"The way I see it," added Roscoe, "we are close to a
brand new century, and I heard tell that pretty soon the

Territories will be a brand new state. It might be called Oklahoma from what I've heard. There are even some guys tryin' to call it Sequoyah after that Cherokee Indian. Who knows? But, fellers, we're makin' history!"

"OK," added Frank. "But I've gotta be honest with you about this Pawnee land. It's pretty wild country over there, and several fugitives find it a soft place to hang out after running from the federal marshal over at Fort Smith."

"I thought our worst enemy would be the Indians," said Anderson.

"No, those folks are pretty friendly these days, especially since we're paying them to live on their land. The big problem is the gangs. Ever hear of the Dalton gang or the Doolin gang?"

"Of course. Who hasn't? We heard about them even up in Vernon County," said Anderson.

"Well, those fellas used to hide out in the caves around Pawnee and raid the settlers."

Anderson wondered, "You say 'used to.' Are they gone now?"

"Yep. The Dalton and Doolin gangs are pretty much a thing of the past, but they knew how to shoot up the town in this last decade. Why, the Doolins robbed trains and banks. Doolin himself took a Pawnee banker hostage after holding up the bank right there on the main street. Doolin was the guy who named Hell Roaring Creek. You'll see that sign as you ride into Pawnee. They say he was asleep near a creek when a big rain came in, and he yelled out, 'It's hell roarin' high.' "

Roscoe scratched his bristly chin and remembered, "Somewhere I saw a picture of that Bill Doolin lyin' in his coffin. It was in 1896, and I recall a U.S. marshal shot him with two shotgun blasts. I counted 20 wounds on his bare chest. That picture like to made me sick."

No one could top that story, so a silence fell over the field.

Anderson felt a chill even though the night was warm. He was glad this was the night Laura and the children were safely asleep in the lodge.

CHAPTER SIX

Entering the lodge, Laura slowly moved to the desk and asked for a room. The manager, sensing a doubtful situation with six people planning to use one room, said, "You've got to pay up front. We don't take any chances here."

"I have the money," said Laura, as she carefully unfastened her shoe and took out two bills.

"Now, you're bringing five children with you. There's just one bed in that room. We don't have extra beds. Take it or leave it." The manager thought he had seen the end of this predicament.

"We'll manage just fine," said Laura.

"Hold on now. There's a problem here. If that little one cries, you'll leave right then. How old is the young-un?"

"My son was three years old last May, and he's very quiet," spoke Laura. Just then Lucy, the little beagle, let out a shrill bark from inside her basket.

Losing all patience, the weary man said, "Oh, no! See the sign? 'No dogs allowed.' That dog might bark all night!"

Laura found her nerve and came back fighting. "I promise you won't hear another sound out of this dog because…."

"Next!" yelled the manager.

Luckily for Laura, there was no one else in line. She continued with "You'll find it hard to believe, but this little beagle had her bark scared out of her by a former owner. She only barks when someone steps on her foot or bumps into her. I must have jabbed her just then."

"Rules are rules. Either get shed of the dog or you all sleep outside."

Laura's sidelong glance at her eldest daughter solved the dilemma. Nelle took the little dog, walked out of the lodge into the darkness, and found her father outside in the park. As she approached the wagon, her father said to Roscoe and Frank, "I knew there'd be a peck of trouble over that dog." Lucy, her tri-color tail wagging, brought laughter to the three men at the campfire.

"So, you not only brought five children, but you let a dog tag along on this journey," chuckled Roscoe. As he saw the sad look on Nelle's face, he added, "And that's a fine-lookin' dog, too."

"Thank you, sir," she whispered. Then Anderson motioned for her to join him as he made room for her and Lucy on the quilt.

After a brief look at Lucy, Roscoe asked, "What kind of dog is that?"

"Well," answered Anderson, "we call her a beagle, but she's more of a mix. She's not only a beagle, but part stray and part friend. She came up to the house one night and never left. My wife saw that shaking dog and was determined to save her. When we started on the trip, there was no question about whether or not to take her along. She is family."

Nelle whispered to her father, "Papa, I'd like to stay out here with you and Lucy. She'll be sad if I go back in there with the others." A nod and smile from Anderson took the sorrowful look out of her eyes.

"You know," laughed Frank, "your little dog there, your Lucy, reminds me of my first dog. We called him Sandy. He was about that size; he kept me warm on cold nights and followed me everywhere."

"Yeah. You don't say," offered Roscoe. "Well, with a name like Sandy, I'll bet he was a brown dog."

"Nope. Gotcha there," answered Frank. "He was a black and white terrier."

"Go on! You don't call a black and white dog 'Sandy' unless you named him during an eclipse. What were you thinkin'?" joked Roscoe.

"Well, we found him out playing in some sand, and the name just happened," quipped Frank.

Recovering from the tale of the oddly-named dog, Roscoe retorted with "Then I feel I owe you the saga of my thirteen cats."

Before anyone could object, Roscoe began with "You see, my first cat had an unsightly blur right on his back that looked like someone dripped paint on the floor. So we called him *Spot*. Then the next spring I found this little gray cat all tousled and dirty out by the pig trough. He was so messy, I thought we'd never get him to lookin' like anything. That was the cat we called *Scruffy*."

"Well," he continued, "two cats couldn't catch all the mice around the place, so we were glad when one mornin' we found this odd-lookin' three-legged cat hobblin' around the barn. You'd say a three-legged cat couldn't amount to much, but this one could nail a mouse just as sure as if he was normal. So we called him *Limpy*."

Just as Roscoe paused to fill his pipe and was starting the tale of the one-eyed cat that came in out of the cold, Frank interrupted and said, "It appears that 'The Deformity Nomenclature' was your method for naming cats."

A puzzled Roscoe stared at Frank, not knowing if he was insulted or just admired, and continued with "Yes. *Cyclops* seemed to fit that one."

Glancing at little Nelle, who was nodding against her father's shoulder, Frank motioned to Roscoe that they should call it a day. Gradually the noises of the other travelers ceased. Horses were bedded for the night, and the tired families had found comfort in their wagons.

After Anderson made sure that Nelle and the dog were secure for the night, he got down to his own worries. "Say, Frank, according to my calculations, we've got about 130 more miles to Pawnee. How far have you folks been able to travel in a typical day?"

Frank paused, took a notebook from his pocket, and responded, "Oh, on a good day, with no trouble on the road, about ten miles. Ideally, if we could have the whole family walking behind the wagon, and just one of us driving, the horses could make better time. As you know, that rarely happens. Then uphill travel is slower, but I guess that ten miles is a good average."

Just then some raucous snoring was heard in the neighborhood of Roscoe. "Looks like we've put our audience to sleep," joked Frank.

"It's just as well," replied Anderson. "We have to talk about some hard times ahead. Have you planned a good route out of here?"

Fumbling in a back pocket, Frank pulled out a crumpled handwritten map. "I've got a neater copy of this in my head, but you can see this one better," he laughed. "What I've done is to plan this trip around the river crossings."

"You bet," said Anderson. "This time of year with the flash flooding in April, we have to be on our guard."

Holding the map toward the fading firelight, Frank said, "Just look at these three rivers: Neosho, Verdigris and Arkansas. What have you heard about them?"

"I know you're aware of the dangers as much as I am, but the bad tales seem to hover around the last one we cross, the Arkansas," answered Anderson. "One family I heard of had a complete wagon turnover just near Blackburn at that Arkansas crossing. They lost everything they had and were forced to walk the last twenty miles into Pawnee."

"Back home there was an old guy named Sam Jeeter who ran the hardware store, and he was nice enough to draw me a map. He swore by the Ralston crossing. He said that just above the town of Ralston there's a place called the 'big bend.' You know how the Arkansas River has that big hump on the maps. Well, it seems that the Osage Indians used to use that spot to cross over for their buffalo hunts. We ought to check that out."

Frank thought for a minute, pulled out his map and drew a straight line. "No. I'd say that fellow was giving good advice as the crow flies, but we're no crows. That would take us deeper into the Cross Timbers' undergrowth and put us too far north from Pawnee. Besides, that route would put us in the Osage Indian country. I think we'd be better off to dip down farther south even though that way would take a few more days."

Anderson sighed and wished there weren't so many opinions to consider. "I guess we'll just take our chances and cross at Blackburn as we planned. We're not on a buffalo hunt, and we sure aren't crows," he chuckled.

Frank had a similar story about the Neosho, which they would come upon at Miami in Indian Territory. "That Neosho is notorious for spring flash floods that wipe out homes in that young town. We'll have to plan an escape route soon if the weather gets bad. If we get there after a series of heavy rains and the water is high, there is a ferry available. We'll be crossing the Neosho north of where it joins with Spring Creek to form the Grand River."

Anderson asked, "What about the Cimarron River? I've heard that it can be treacherous with its sandy channel."

"Not only that, but it is almost as wide as the Arkansas. However, we won't be going that far south. My biggest fear is the overturning of a wagon. So, let's talk more about how that thing won't happen to us. I think I have a route here that will serve us well," whispered Frank as he realized they had talked far into the night. The two men felt a sense of accomplishment in knowing they agreed on a plan for the rest of the trip. The last sound heard was a chorus of crickets singing a lonely concert under the stars.

CHAPTER SEVEN

Feeling a wet nose nuzzling her arm, Nelle woke to see her furry friend. The beagle was pushing toward a warmer spot in the crumpled quilt. Nelle was remembering last night's dinner as she pulled herself out of the wagon and very softly walked to the campfire to encourage the embers and warmth with the possibility of breakfast.

The men were still enjoying the last of their slumber and were oblivious to any outside activity.

As Nelle was engrossed in finding a long stick for restoring last night's fire, a smiling lady from another wagon approached, carrying her cooking gear.

She whispered, "I'd love to share this campfire of yours. My name is Jane Barnes."

Nelle felt a surge of kindness as she looked at the newcomer's face. "I'm Nelle from the other wagon over there. My family is heading out west and...."

Just then, a hungry Lucy sniffed the bacon and was about to knock a frying pan out of Jane's hands.

"Oh, I do believe you are traveling with a very friendly pet," laughed Jane.

"Not to mention hungry," added Nelle as she rescued the pan with one hand and grasped her dog with the other. "I am so sorry about our dog. She gets a little anxious at meal times."

By this time, Laura and her four other children were walking back from their night at the inn. Before they could share their adventures with their papa, the Barnes children climbed down from their wagon.

Frank moved quickly to his wife's side and took charge of some quick introductions. "Barnes family, meet the Mansfields. We're headed the same way to the same town, and I feel we're going to be the best of friends."

Seven children and a frisky dog began to make their own introductions. Nine-year-old Hazel Barnes and seven-year-old Fred Barnes were a bit overwhelmed by the five new children, but they were delighted by the antics of the ever-friendly Lucy. When Hazel tossed a ball to the dog, the children came to join in the fun.

Jane and Laura immediately started a breakfast from their families' grub boxes, and found a welcome companionship they had missed for the past few weeks.

"So, you folks are on your way to Pawnee County?" asked Jane.

"That's right. We've left our home in search of a new land," answered Laura, trying to sound brave.

"I know what you're feeling. The hardest part for us was to leave our parents back there in Carthage. They were opposed to having us move so far and especially to see their two grandchildren leave. Did your folks try to keep you from heading out west?"

"No," answered Laura. "My husband's people are in Virginia. He had already broken away to become a farmer in Missouri."

"Well, what about your parents? Didn't they oppose your decision?"

"No," continued Laura. "I am an orphan. I never knew my parents, so my early life was spent in an orphanage back in Schell City."

"Oh, I'm so sorry. What an insensitive question."

"Not at all, Jane. How would you know? I had a very happy life there."

From across the way, Frank Barnes yelled, "How is the breakfast coming over there? It looks like we have two good cooks today. It should be twice as good!"

He led the hungry crowd to the fireside and motioned for the mothers to be seated as he and Anderson proceeded to serve the breakfast.

As the two families gathered for the breakfast picnic, the two mothers had a chance for more exchange of information. The questions flew back and forth. How did you decide what to bring and what to leave behind? Has anyone been sick on the trail? How is your family bathing and washing clothes? How will we live in a dugout?

The two fathers had a chance for similar questions.

Anderson began with "My life has always been involved in farming. My father was a rancher back in Virginia, but he also was the town veterinarian for lack of anyone else nearby who knew anything about animal care. He was not an official animal doctor, but he had learned how to heal sick animals through necessity."

"How could he learn enough to be able to treat all those diseases?" asked Frank.

"Well, he read everything he could get his hands on about disease in cattle and horses. I worked with him as soon as I was old enough. By the time I was born, my parents were getting on in years. I was the last of the brood, and they were both over forty when I appeared. My eight siblings showed no interest or ability to shoe a horse or assist in the birth of a calf, so I fell into that job. I dearly love animals, so I am another guy who learned animal doctoring just by doing it. What was your life like in Carthage?"

Frank explained, "I trained to be a history and science teacher. I was especially interested in botany. However, all that time that I was teaching that stuff, I just wished I could be out there digging in the soil and seeing crops grow. My father was a farmer, so I'm not going into this thing blind, and I'm not afraid of hard work."

"It was hard to leave home, though, because our parents fought with us about moving. I guess the only argument I had that my mother fell for was the fact that her older brother, Travis, lives in Pawnee. She figured he would look out for us. He is a lawyer out there. He and his wife, Sadie, built up a pretty good-sized ranch north of town. Sadie died a year ago, and Uncle Travis is having to adjust to her loss. I want you to meet him when we get out there. Somehow I think the two of you would really hit it off."

"Sounds good to me. How are your two children handling this wagon travel?" asked Anderson.

"Pretty good. Hazel is a good sport and seems to look on it all as a great adventure. She is keeping a diary and wants to pick all the wild flowers along the way and press them in a book. Fred has his sullen moods. He hated to leave his Carthage friends. I fear he may have more trouble adjusting to a new life than will Hazel."

"Isn't it strange how two children in the same family can be so different? Our five children are not alike at all. You'll see what I mean when you've been around us more. The two redheads, Daisy and Owen, are the fun-loving pair, and the three brunettes, Nelle, Opal and Donna are my serious ones. That Nelle is a born leader. Opal is docile and kind, and Donna is the creative one. No two alike!"

"Uh oh! My Jane is giving me that look. I've talked right through the cleanup time. Let's get this wagon train ready for its next adventure! Say. Maybe you could take a look at my Molly's left front hoof. She has been favoring that one. Maybe a stray stone lodged up in there somewhere?"

So Anderson nodded and began to check the hooves of all the horses. Laura had loaded the grub box, the children were checked over in readiness for the next ride, and both fathers felt a sense of kinship over their traveling companions.

CHAPTER EIGHT

From Joplin the two families formed a caravan and followed a well-worn trail that helped them travel faster than before. By noon the two prairie schooners had arrived at the line marking the crossing from Missouri to Indian Territory.

Seeing the wagons leave the familiar homeland, Laura wondered what changes she would find in this new land. At the northeast corner of Indian Territory were seven Indian settlements. In the midst of these was the town of Miami.

Anderson had prepared his family for the changes just ahead. He cautioned, "Now you need to be on guard for the Indians you'll see. Above all, don't stare at their unusual clothing. Some of them will be in outfits like ours, but others cling to their old ways. Remember that we are under different laws than we had back home. Tribal law gives the advantage to the tribe members. We mustn't violate any of their rules. There are even some Indians who don't want us in their land, so keep to yourself. We are just crossing over into another territory. There is a big difference in passing through and trespassing."

All of those warnings just kindled the imaginations of the children.

Opal said, "I've heard that scalps sometimes disappear in Indian attacks."

Daisy asked, "What do they want with our hair? Will it grow back? Would they like my red hair or Nelle's brown hair?"

Momma tried to change the subject and hoped no one would explain to Daisy that scalping and cutting hair were not the same.

In the distance Anderson saw teepees in a circle and was thankful that the well-worn trail kept far to the left of the settlement. Then he saw Jane Barnes in the wagon ahead of him signaling a time to stop. With a pull on the brake lever, Anderson brought the rear wheels to an abrupt halt. Frank led his wagon to a smooth stop.

Quickly the children jumped from their wagons to stretch their legs. They were soon involved in a game of fox and geese with Jane and Laura joining in the fun. Lucy stretched her four legs and chased a frightened squirrel up a tree.

"What do you say we find a place to camp for the night?" asked Frank. "We are just outside of Miami, and we need provisions for the next leg through the Cherokee Territory."

"I'd welcome a breather here," admitted Anderson. "Tomorrow we'll be crossing the Neosho River, so we need to be at our best. Let's get some information on the depth of the river here. Didn't I hear there is a ferry crossing available?"

"Sure thing," answered Frank, "but the cost might be something to consider."

Already the mothers had decided they could set up a campfire for dinner and hoped the men would agree to spend the night in that very spot.

"I wouldn't argue with staying here," said Frank. "It looks like open country, and no one is telling us to move. Let's cook what's left in the grub box, and tomorrow we'll fill up in town."

Just then two covered wagons approached from the same trail. The front wagon was driven by a tired-looking woman, carefully shielding her face with an attractive sunbonnet. Behind her was an even larger wagon driven by a robust-looking man. Lucy greeted the travelers with her friendly barking.

"Hi, little dog, and greetings, strangers," called the man. "May the Taylors join you for the evening? We're road-weary and willing to share some grub."

"Of course you can join and share," answered Frank. "We'd love to compare notes and plans with you over supper."

Very soon three pioneer women began cooking over an impromptu fire. The game of fox and geese had died down, but a new game of blindman's bluff was just beginning.

Millie Taylor offered her wild sand plums and sausages. Jane Barnes found leftover biscuits and honey. Laura Mansfield had potatoes to bake on the hot coals and coffee to wash it all down. While the women worked together, Laura seemed to feel a kinship around the fire. Without putting her thoughts into words, she felt she knew the hardships that each one had endured to get this far on her own journey. However, there were questions that had to be answered.

Laura asked, "Where are you folks from, and what is your destination?" Laura had already told about the Land Run and the aftermath of leaving Missouri and renting land in Pawnee County.

Millie was astounded. "Well, we just started from Joplin to head out for our 160 acres that Norris won in the Cherokee Strip Run of '93. He lived on his claim for five years, just as the government required. Now he owns the land outright. He came back to Joplin, wooed and won me, and we are heading out to start a new life on our own land. My friends thought our romance would never last at such a distance. We were high school sweethearts, and then he heard about this great chance to claim 160 acres. We continued to keep up with each other writing. First it was just an occasional note. After three years he seemed to be making a go of the frontier life, and I thought maybe I might be able to live out in the territory. So I just started making a hope chest. You two probably did the same thing. I embroidered tea towels and crocheted blankets, just in case he ever really asked me to marry him. Of course, I wasn't getting any younger, and my folks had just about given up on my ever finding anyone with a real future. Well, when he finally finished up that five years that the law required and actually had built a log cabin, I just knew he'd be wanting me to be his wife. You'd better believe that my folks were shocked when he came back to Joplin and even brought a ring. So, here I am, an old married woman, twenty-three years old, with a hope chest full of good stuff."

Jane fought the sinking feeling at hearing of such a story and found the courage to ask about their wagons. "Don't you agree it was hard to decide what to bring along to start a home in the territory? A wagon doesn't allow you to pack all you want to, does it?"

"Absolutely!" said Millie. "That's why we had to bring two wagons. I had to be very selective, so I just brought the bare necessities. Over there I have two trunks of clothes and my little necessities and my grandfather clock and the treadle sewing machine. Of course, I had to have my dishes and my cooking utensils and my hope chest."

"Well, what's in that other wagon?" asked Laura.

"Oh, that's Norris' wagon. Since he has already spent five years roughing it, he could be more sure of what he needed. There's a sod plow, a rake, a scythe, two hoes, and four kitchen chairs. Then, of course, a rocking chair and a large iron Dutch oven on four legs with a heavy lid. I just couldn't keep house without that Dutch oven!"

Several moments of silence followed as the other two women struggled to find the correct response.

"Did you have any trouble getting stuck in the mud with all the weight in that second wagon?" asked Jane out of desperation.

"Of course not. See those two oxen that are pulling each wagon? We knew horses couldn't handle all our belongings. So far, we've had a marvelous journey. I just hope my skin isn't damaged by the intense sunshine. I am very fair as you have no doubt noticed."

Just then Norris Taylor approached the group of women and cautioned, "Don't let Millie do all the talking, ladies. She loves to gab. That's what attracted me to her." Laura assured Norris that everyone had a chance to talk and invited the men to grab a plate and serve themselves. Soon all thirteen travelers had gathered around the campfire, found a seat and fed themselves.

While the women cleaned the supper dishes and repacked their food supplies, the men compared plans for their upcoming travel.

"Norris, how are you planning to take your wagons across the Neosho River?" asked Anderson. "We've heard that river can be treacherous any time of year."

"I'm surprised you'd even ask," laughed Norris. "My heavy loads and oxen are going on that ferry I've heard about. Why try to save a little money on a risky crossing? Think what a loss I'd have if all that farm equipment washed down the Neosho into the Grand River! No, sir. I'm counting on a safe ride via ferry, and the cost is no problem."

"Well," added Frank, "you do have a sizeable load. I guess it's each man for himself at this point."

"Anyway," continued the confident Norris, "we're stopping here for a while to rest. Millie is a bit under the weather, and I have a cousin in Miami who will be glad to see us. He has just built a two-story house, and has plenty of room for us. He runs the bank in Miami."

"Oh" said Frank. "Then I guess we won't be traveling with you as you continue to. . . where did you say you were heading?"

"It's our 160 acres in Pawnee County, out south of town. I've already built the log cabin, and I even have a hired hand living there while I'm away. I had him plant corn and squash two weeks ago after the last frost. You said you both are heading in that direction, but what is your actual destination?"

Frank replied, "Honestly, Anderson and I tried for land in the Cherokee Strip Run, but misfortune was ours. You probably remember that not everyone made a killing that day. So we'll be sharecropping for a while, but that's all right. We have an Indian landlord who has treated us well, and our hopes are high."

"Pawnee County is our destination," continued Anderson. "We'll be three miles north of town. Drop by anytime. Our log cabins are in the future, but our dugouts or maybe even soddies will be fine for the first year."

Stunned by their story, the lucky landowner said, "Well, I'll be! Just think of that. We three guys were all out there, sweating and struggling on that hot September day in '93. Wasn't that a mob of people out there at noon when the bugles sounded! I guess we'll never forget that day!"

As the campfire died down, so did the talking, and each of the three families retired to their wagons. As Laura was falling asleep, she wondered how luck would stay with the Taylors and particularly how they would ever get those heavy wagons across the treacherous Arkansas River at the end of the trip.

CHAPTER NINE

As the sun began to appear on the horizon, Anderson and Frank met at the remains of last night's campfire to plan the crossing on the Neosho.

"Would 'pennywise and pound foolish' be Norris' label for our ignoring the ferry?" asked Anderson.

"Probably, but you know I wouldn't put my family at risk. I really think we can make it today. There's a shallow stretch a mile south of here that the guy at the livery stable told me about last night. I'm ready," responded Frank. "How about a hike down to the river's edge to see what we're up against?"

Anderson agreed, but he took time to inform Laura of their plans.

"Why don't you take Lucy with you?" she suggested. "She needs a chance to run free."

So the two men and a dog inspected the territory. The early signs of spring were everywhere. Aromatic weeds filled the air with sweetness. Henbit and wildflowers made both men wish their crops were already in the ground. Lucy found some wild baby rabbits to chase along the way. She soon gave up the chase and began to chew on wild onions under a blackjack tree.

Watching the tail-wagging dog, Frank asked, "Why did you name her Lucy?"

"Oh, that was Laura's idea. It's kind of complicated, but it explains a lot about my wife. She used to think that she'd like to teach school. I think it's all because of her favorite English teacher, Miss Rodey. That woman made poetry come alive for Laura. I never could understand that stuff myself. It was just a puzzle to me. Why couldn't they just tell it in plain language? But Laura loved it, especially Wordsworth."

"Hold it," interrupted Frank. "What ever happened to my question about Lucy?"

"I'm just about to that part. It was William Wordsworth who gave her the idea. You see, he wrote some poems about a sweet young girl named Lucy, and people have wondered about her ever since. That was 100 years ago, but the mystery continues. Some people think Lucy was a girl who died and was dearly loved by the poet. All I remember was this one line, 'She dwelt among the untrodden ways.' Doesn't it have a nice ring to it?"

Frank replied, "It kind of sounds like what your Lucy is doing right now chasing that rabbit though the sumac bushes!"

"Well, you could say all of us are following untrodden ways this month. Anyway, that night when this sad, wet little dog appeared at our door all hungry and alone, Laura quoted that line and then welcomed our Lucy."

"Thanks. I didn't know you knew so much about a poet when I asked you that simple question," laughed Frank.

"I've heard about those Lucy poems for quite a while. Just be glad you didn't ask Laura. She probably would have sat you down while she read all the poems to you."

"Just to keep the record straight, friend, I have to point out that we aren't the first ones to set foot here. About 800 years ago there were Wichita and Osage Indians who migrated to this very area. Then later, as I recall, the Chickamauga Cherokees were in control. And don't forget that in 1874 the Pawnees arrived. So, Laura can wax poetic and talk about the area as the 'untrodden ways' but many feet have walked here before Mr. William Wordsworth or our families or that little mystery girl Lucy were ever thought of."

"I keep forgetting I am in the presence of a history teacher. Thanks for setting me straight, Frank. Now it's up to you to explain all that to my wife," chuckled Anderson.

Eventually, Lucy led the men to the edge of the Neosho River where it was time to make a decision.

"Let's just walk through the river as far as we can and then decide," said Frank.

The slowly-moving current was a good sign as the men tested the possibilities. Several sand banks in the distance gave them hope.

"Let's do it!" said Anderson. Lucy was trying out her water skills and loving the new adventure.

By the time the men had returned to their families, a hearty breakfast was ready, and the seven children were involved in hide-and-seek. The early morning activities caused everyone to eat well.

"We're feeling good about a safe crossing today," Anderson announced to the whole group. "Frank and I tested the place, and we just need to tread carefully."

Jane suggested to Laura, "Let's make sure everything is tied down and the most precious items stowed below the others."

Laura nodded but wondered what changes could be done at this point since she had already arranged the family's possessions that way. The wagon could only hold the most needed supplies and treasured keepsakes. Those decisions had been made before they left home. Nevertheless, she checked on the family Bible, each child's favorite toy, the sewing kit, the family photo box, the peony plants, and her book of poetry.

The children were excited over their first river crossing. Nelle thought they could all hold on to each other for safety. Opal wanted to ride with her new friend Hazel in the Barnes' wagon, but her request was denied. Donna was crying because she couldn't swim, and Daisy and Owen wanted to get wet in the pretty water.

After an hour of preparation, each family had organized itself for the trip to the river's edge. The sun was at their backs, there was a gentle breeze, and their spirits were good. Blaze and Belle led the way, cautiously trying the cold springtime river water. Soon the horses were at home in the new environment.

Anderson whispered to his children, "Keep calm now. No yelling or even loud talking. We mustn't scare the horses. Our safety depends on our four-legged friends."

Then very softly the father began to sing, "Come to me, my little gypsy sweetheart." Laura instinctively put Lucy in her lap and began stroking her head. Soon the little dog was snoring contentedly.

Halfway across, the horses encountered the sand bank. Startled at first, they quickly adjusted and then readjusted to the deeper water on the other side. The opposite bank was a little higher than hoped for, but Anderson's careful handling eased the wagon up to safety. Very soon the Barnes family had achieved a successful crossing with nothing lost in the attempt.

Frank Barnes hugged each child as the two families disembarked for a brief rest.

"I am so proud and thankful that you children kept calm all the way across the river. There are grownups who couldn't have behaved as well as you did."

Fred admitted, "I almost yelled out one time when that big catfish came alongside our wagon! Mama had to clap her hand across my mouth."

"I wanted to yell out to Hazel when we saw you at the midway point, but I knew better," said Donna.

"The horses needed all of us keeping still. They really earned their oats this time," added Jane.

"Maybe Millie and Norris Taylor will have a more carefree crossing on that ferry, but they can't have as much fun as we had," laughed Laura.

CHAPTER TEN

Traveling south from Miami, the wagons avoided major water crossings and enjoyed clement weather. Nights were spent with the two families sharing stories, examining the stars of the spring sky and making more plans for their new life.

Anderson entertained the children with several different star stories each night. His best ones were Orion and his three-starred belt and Draco the Dragon. He claimed that he was finding his way by the North Star, just as the sailors did. Owen loved to hear how the very stars he was looking at had burnt out long ago, but their light was still reaching the earth. Those stories never seemed to grow old.

After a week, the two families saw the sign "Chelsea, Indian Territory." Laura and Jane were relieved to arrive at this point because the men had planned a day's rest here.

"Yes," announced Anderson, "this is about as far south as our map says we need to go. This must be about at the 37th parallel. We'll travel west to Hominy and Blackburn and be ready to cross the mighty Arkansas."

The men had stopped their wagons and were conferring about plans for the night. With three more hours of daylight they saw the chance to let their wives and children tour the town and shop for needed supplies. A city park with several wagons parked for the night was a welcome sight. As they brought their wagons to a good resting place, another man invited them to join his campfire.

"Always room for more. Welcome to Chelsea," said a red-haired man who was stirring a large pot of soup.

Frank, glad to find a friendly face, said, "My buddy Anderson will join us in a while. He's overseeing his family on a search for provisions. What can you tell me about this place?"

"Well, first of all, my name is Brogdon, Luther Brogdon."

"Hi there, Luther. I'm Frank Barnes."

"Nice to meet you. I'll tell you what I know, and I'm a newcomer here myself. It seems this town is recently established. See that store over there? Well, a feller told me it was the first store, and the date on the front says 1881. Some Delaware Indian is the proprietor. From the looks of that main street you can see the other folks got busy with filling in the gaps. Right there is a grist mill. Then there is a fine-looking bank on the next corner, just where a bank should be. There's even an opera house a block up the street. Imagine that!"

"With all that information, I'm tempted to stay right here, but we have to move on," sighed Frank.

"You folks might want to think on that. I haven't told you the best part," said Brogdon with a sly grin.

"O.K. I'm ready."

"Well, sir, you might want to know that just a few years back, I think it was in 1889, a guy struck oil right here in Chelsea. They say it was the first oil well in Indian Territory. That's why I'm staying. My hopes are high because I'm not afraid of hard work. My cabin is about a mile from here, but I do my cooking in this park."

Frank and his new friend Luther were pleased to see Anderson and the rest of the travelers return. As the sun was setting, the mothers prepared a meal from the fresh food found in the general store. As Anderson and Frank tended the horses, they shared their news about the new town. The Barnes children were excited over the entertaining trip up and down the main street.

"Why can't we just stay here?" asked Fred. "I could have a lot of fun in those stores."

"Me, too," added Hazel. "Everything's so new. There's a drug store, a general store, and toys in the window of another store. I'm tired of eating wild plums and bathing in a creek."

"Hold on now," warned Frank. "Sure, this sounds like a great town. I just learned that someone struck oil here. That made me want to hang around too, but remember this. We have a place to live in Pawnee County."

"What about that oil here?" asked Nelle.

"You know what? Oil belongs to the guy who owns the land, and we aren't that guy," said Frank.

"Sure, and who knows? There probably will be oil out in Pawnee. I just have a feeling there will be. Someday we'll own land there and who knows what!" said Anderson.

All this talk had put Lucy into a deep sleep with its accompanying snores. Soon the families had bedded down and let their snores join the nighttime concert.

Starting out the next morning, the Mansfield wagon was unusually quiet. The previous day's excitement had left the children weary and content with a morning nap. Laura, however, was more alert than usual. All morning she had experienced a strange feeling that trouble was near.

Then it happened. Owen noticed a slithering in the toy box.

"Mama!" he cried. "A big worm is playing with the blocks!"

As she saw a large snake burrowing for cover, she screamed, "Anderson, you've got to stop NOW!"

Frustrated by the unexpected command, Papa yelled back, "I can't just stop a wagon like that! What's wrong with you?"

Now Laura was crying and pulling the children away from the wooden box.

"It's a snake, one of the worst ones," she sobbed.

Anderson had two phobias in his life: snakes and the feel of velvet. At that moment, the velvet didn't seem so bad. He pulled back on the reins, coaxing his horses as calmly as his fear would allow.

"Hang on to a pole," he warned. The family knew what to do. They grasped the center pole to withstand the thrust of the quick stop. However, one gunny sack of the Chelsea potatoes took a flying leap out the back.

"Everybody out, now!" yelled Anderson.

Scrambling over the top of their belongings, they hit the ground. But the brave father hovered over the toy box until he heard the tell-tale rattle. Whoosh! He threw the wooden box out the back of the wagon, with blocks going everywhere. There on the floor of the wagon lay a three-foot rattlesnake ready to strike. Miraculously, Anderson had found his rifle, and he fired one shot at the head of the snake. The danger was over.

The brave father took a deep breath to calm himself. Then he taught the children a very important lesson with his snake speech.

"There are two snakes to fear in this part of the land. They are the rattlesnakes and copperheads. You heard the rattle this time."

The front of Laura's blouse was wet with tears of fear as she huddled her family close to her. Lucy sniffed at the dead snake, then lost interest. The children didn't have to be told to check their bedding each night for the rest of the journey.

CHAPTER ELEVEN

The wagons were stopped at a resting spot in western Osage County. After a hard day of avoiding the dense growth of vegetation in the Cross Timbers area, Anderson and Frank welcomed a chance to make some last-minute plans. Sitting beside the smoldering campfire, they watched the last vista of sunset fade into the horizon.

"Frank, you never told me how you found this farmland in the Oklahoma Territory."

"Well, my Uncle Travis wrote me about an Indian he had come across at the Pawnee Agency. I think I told you that Travis is a lawyer at Pawnee. One of his clients is an Indian named White Eagle, who wants to rent his allotment."

"Now wait a minute!" interrupted Anderson. "You don't mean you are renting from White Eagle, too?"

"You mean he is your Pawnee landlord?"

The two men were speechless, but only for a moment.

"Then, we're not just neighbors; we're next-door neighbors! And my question," said the excited Frank, "is how did you find him?"

"Well, I saw an advertisement in the Schell City paper and answered it. The man seemed to be an honest person. No money has changed hands. I guess

I'm taking a big risk, but it just sounded like a great deal," admitted Anderson. "Now, let me ask you about something that has been bothering me. Is White Eagle really renting us good land? Or does he think this land of his isn't any good for farming? I have been wondering about all this red dirt we have encountered lately. It sure doesn't look like that rich, dark, loamy soil we left back in Missouri."

"Let me set you straight. Just because he wants to rent us his land doesn't mean it's unsuitable for farming. Remember those Pawnee Indians were a hunting tribe back in Nebraska. When the government moved them down to the territory in 1875, they didn't know how to farm and didn't want to learn how. They are more than happy to make money from those of us who know how to till the soil."

"Then let me get this straight. This Indian will rent his land to us, and your Uncle Travis is going to make it all legal?"

"Sure," replied Frank. "Uncle Travis knows the law, and he has handled several of these Indian deals. And don't worry about red dirt you've been finding on your wagon wheels. Pawnee County is part of the Red Bed Plains. It's good land. So, rest assured that it will bring in a crop. That red dirt means that there is iron oxide here, and Pawnee is known for great farming land, especially the rich bottom land along the Arkansas River. What's more, this particular allotment is just three miles north of town. Of course, it would have been better to get the land free in the Land Run, but we both know how that turned out for us."

"O.K. I see you have been doing your research. But tell me how you plan to pay the rent. White Eagle didn't make any of this clear in his letters to me," admitted Anderson.

Frank tried to put a positive slant on the details as he saw the worry lines forming on Anderson's forehead. "White Eagle wants earnest money up front. That's only fair. So I plan to sell one of these fine horses I have with me for around 50 dollars. I can make do with one horse for farming for a while."

Anderson interrupted, "Then how do you plan to pay the rest?"

"I am calling myself a sharecropper. Do you find that word offensive?" asked Frank.

"Nope. Laura and I have already described ourselves that way. I think that word describes our position pretty well. A late spring crop could start to bring in some profit, weather permitting. But I sure worry about the stories I've heard where one hailstorm could wipe out a whole crop for some of these settlers."

Frank continued, "Sure. It's going to be hard, but we're both young, our wives can work alongside us, and we have our children to help us. You're lucky to have a wife who seems to be healthy enough to help you in the fields."

Frank added, "We can call ourselves sharecroppers or tenant farmers, but Uncle Travis says the term in Pawnee right now is share tenants. We really have three choices on our share. We can keep two-thirds or three-fourths of our crop, depending on how much rent we want to pay. However, if we pay cash rental, we can keep all the proceeds of our crops. White Eagle is a very helpful and understanding man. You'll see what I mean."

"Let's pray we all stay well and strong," Anderson said softly.

Meanwhile, Laura and Jane were finding a chance to make their own plans. Seeing the men chatting at the campfire, they sat on the seat of the Mansfield wagon, watching their children playing a game of leap frog, and shared their concerns about educating the youngsters.

"What have you heard from your relatives in Pawnee about schools?" asked Laura.

Jane reassuringly replied, "Pawnee already has a school near our farmland. It is called Oak Grove. The children go there from grades one through eight."

"How big is this Oak Grove?" Laura asked.

"It is only one room. One teacher teaches all the grades, but they have good reports on how well the school works. The teacher has been there two years, and she really knows how to handle those students. They use the McGuffey Readers. I heard those books include the classic writers and promote patriotism and good morals. They read Shakespeare, Dickens and even Washington Irving. By the way, Irving came through this area back in the 1830's. Maybe our children will get to read about what he thought of this rough terrain. Your Nelle and Opal are old enough to start school as soon as we arrive. Our Hazel and Fred can join them."

"How does one teacher keep track of all the different levels of instruction in one room?" asked Laura.

"She has them doing seven different assignments based on what book they can handle, all the way from the Primer to the Sixth Reader. You'll be amazed!"

Jane started to mention her fear of the typhoid fever that had taken two local children at Oak Grove last winter, but she couldn't find the courage to warn Laura. Suddenly a shot was heard beside the campfire.

Frantically, Laura and Jane jumped down from the wagon and ran to the fireside, gathering the children around them. Calmly, Anderson cautioned them to stay back. He motioned to the clump of blackjack trees ten feet away from them.

"What happened? Where's my husband?" cried Jane.

"Everything's O.K. We heard some kind of wild animal in there, but I think the danger is over," Anderson assured them.

Another shot was heard. Then all was quiet. The three peered into the dark overhanging trees to see Frank, shotgun over his shoulder, emerging from a forest of red cedars. Hair in his eyes and blood on his plaid shirt, he still had his grin as he said, "That's one mountain lion that won't be bothering our horses tonight. I hope if he has any pals, they have headed south."

Shaking with fear, the women were glad to return to the wagons and to their brave husbands.

As he started to fall asleep that night, Anderson remembered why he was glad to be leaving the Cross Timbers area with its heavy growth of blackjacks, red cedars and undergrowth of briars, a perfect hiding place for mountain lions. Losing a horse at this point in the journey would have left them defenseless.

He kept mulling over the comment from Frank about Laura being strong enough to help him in the field. That asset was going to be invaluable to him. Then there was Nelle, already strong for her age, and able to lift almost as well as Laura. How would a man survive without family members beside him?

Soon some threatening clouds hurrying across the sky turned off the light of the brightest star, and a soft rain played a calming melody on the canvas coverings overhead. Anderson tried to find himself falling asleep, but his thoughts were playing games in his head.

CHAPTER TWELVE

After an hour of lying in the comfort of the gentle rain, Anderson knew he had to continue the conversation about the crops. Cautiously he crept from his sleeping family and reappeared at the side of the Barnes' wagon. To his surprise, Frank had returned to the fireside and was drawing a map in the dirt by the dying fireside. Anderson took out his notebook and started drawing a farming blueprint.

"I couldn't sleep either until I saw this plan on paper. We each plan to rent forty acres, and I need to see how we can survive on that small a plot."

"Sure," whispered Frank. "Those forty acres will provide enough for each family, but the profit will be meager. We just have to scrimp and save and hope for a larger farm in the near future."

"Then let's make a list right now," said Anderson. We need to know the best crops for this time of the year. By the time we get our fields plowed, it will be too late for spring oats. But sweet corn could be our best crop. We could have a fine harvest by October."

"Don't forget potatoes. We can still plant those in April," added Frank. "And since you mentioned corn, I'd like to try some kaffir corn. It's drought tolerant and has so many uses. I heard that you can even grind it and make coffee."

In the firelight, Frank didn't see the frowning face of Anderson as he thought of that kaffir coffee. Anderson was studying his drawing and sighing, "I'd love to try a few acres of broomcorn, too. I've heard there's a need for that crop out in Pawnee."

Frank chuckled softly at the thought of seven hungry people trying to raise a crop that no one could eat. He suggested, "Maybe for the first year you should think about feeding your children instead of sweeping the floor."

Anderson saw no humor in his idea and informed him that he had heard Pawnee had a specialty store that featured broomcorn brooms.

"O.K., friend," said Frank. "You grow broomcorn, and I'll try kaffir corn. At least we'll have coffee while we sweep our dirt floors!"

In a calmer voice, Anderson suggested, "Well, one thing we can agree on is winter wheat."

"Oh, yeah. It's probably the major cash crop in Pawnee County, according to what Uncle Travis has told me. Let's plan to get our ground ready for that wheat planting in late September."

By this time, the ashes were barely emitting any light, and Anderson's notes were completely illegible. However, the ideas of crops and field layout were permanently etched in his mind. The two farmers stepped softly back to their families, thankful that their future seemed more secure.

CHAPTER THIRTEEN

Early morning light was scant on Tuesday as the two families prepared for the last day of travel at the end of their long trip.

Scanning the sky, Anderson grumbled to himself, "Those clouds are full of mischief."

As the wind was picking up and rustling the few leaves on the cottonwoods overhead, he quietly left the comfort of the schooner and headed toward the Barnes family wagon.

"Psst, Frank. Are you awake yet?"

Pulling on his overalls, Frank softly stepped down to confer with his friend.

"Not until you messed with my dreams. What's so important at this early hour?" he asked.

"I just wonder if you think we should go ahead and cross the Arkansas with this ugly weather coming out of the west," questioned Anderson.

"Well, doggone you. Here we are almost to Blackburn, just a day's distance from Pawnee, and you want to slow us down. It's not like we're fording a stream. Remember we heard there's a new bridge up ahead. We've seen dark clouds before, but that's no sure sign we'll have a deluge."

"Frank, I want to agree with you, but I have a sinking feeling that we should wait this one out. We are up against the widest river yet, and a flash flood could be a disaster," Anderson warned.

"O.K. Let's just not alarm the others. We'll enjoy this sunrise, have a good breakfast and decide after that. But keep calm."

While the men were talking, Laura had started the campfire, and the appealing smell of coffee wafted toward them. Fat biscuits were cooking in the big black skillet.

"Hope there's some apple butter left for our last day of sojourn," called her husband, trying his best to look secure in his plans.

"Papa, don't you think we've got a big storm coming up?" asked the vigilant Nelle as she saw her father approaching.

"Could just be some low-drifting clouds playing pranks on us. Help your mother find some meat for these hungry folks," suggested Anderson. Glancing above a row of eastern red cedars, he saw black clouds scudding across the sky.

By this time, the Barnes children and the Mansfield children were gathering around the fireside along with the frisky Lucy. The two wives were especially excited as they talked about the end of their trek.

Stirring the coffee, Laura said, "What is the most amazing thing about this trip to you, Jane?"

"We haven't lost anything or anybody on this month-long journey. I thought we'd have to toss out some of our belongings halfway here when the horses got tired, but everything is intact. My beloved peony plants even made it this far to start a new life in new soil. I am still hanging on to the sassafras roots so we can make the blood-clearing tea this spring. Remember all the warnings we had about the coyotes and the gangs that marauded other covered wagons?"

"Yes," answered Laura, "but my biggest fear was having a wagon overturn when we forded those two rivers, especially the Neosho. What with the spring flooding and all, we could have lost everything, even a family member. You've heard the old stories."

"Oh my, yes. But now we're about to enter Pawnee County just on the other side of this big river, and in a few miles we will see our new homeplace," said Jane. "I couldn't be happier."

In spite of the humid morning, there was a feeling of joy and anticipation that surrounded the two families as they enjoyed their final breakfast on the road. Gradually, tiny raindrops began peppering the fire and the crowd. Then the raindrops stopped, indicating a possible day of little intermittent showers. Just as Frank was about to tell Anderson they should still forge ahead, the rain came down much harder. As lightning streaked across the horizon followed by a clap of thunder, the women and children quickly packed up their cooking supplies and headed to the wagons. Outside, under the protection of a giant post oak tree, Anderson and John had to make a quick decision.

"Look," shouted Frank. "We are about to have a real downpour, and we're just about a half mile from that Blackburn bridge." Another loud thunder clap sounded, and shrieks from the children were heard. "We'd better get high behind and cross over that bridge now!"

"Are you saying," interrupted Anderson, "that we should head into a possible storm and cross a possibly raging river? We could even be hit by lightning! You're crazy!"

"I'm afraid we don't have a choice. It's now or never, and we'll have to take our chances." Another much louder thunder clap sounded. This time it cracked a nearby tree that fell with a resounding thud. "I'm heading out. See you on the other side!" yelled Frank as he ran to his family's wagon.

By now the west wind and heavy rain were pelting both men as they ran to join their families. Quickly they took off in the midst of the downpour. The Barnes family arrived at the bridge first and had a successful crossing into Blackburn.

Inside the Mansfield wagon, Laura hurried to secure the children and dog.

"Nelle, you'll be the anchor. Now everyone must hold tight to Nelle and to each other. Just as soon as we get across to Blackburn, we'll all be dry and warm."

"But Mama," cried Opal, "who can hold onto these books of yours?"

"Nelle, you sit on this poetry book, and I'll be sitting on the Bible."

Laura hurried to take her place on the seat beside Anderson, who was gripping the reins with all his strength. Grasping the rough board seat, she felt the family Bible beneath her and prayed that it would help their safe arrival in the new land. She was so glad Anderson had treated the wagon's canvas top with linseed oil to make it more waterproof.

The sky had become so dark with clouds that it looked like nighttime. Another thunder clap scared everyone, especially the horses. Little Owen cried the loudest and wouldn't stop. Laura was trying not to cry as she told the children to be brave. Quickly the wind picked up and was blowing the rain sideways, breaking oak limbs and soaking all the belongings. "So much for the waterproof cover on this wagon," muttered Anderson.

"Mama, make the rain stop!" begged Opal, as she pulled at her mother's skirt.

"I only wish I could," replied Laura. "Just be glad we're almost there."

Soon the sound of rushing water warned Anderson that the long-awaited Arkansas River was just ahead. He managed to coax the reluctant horses onto the new bridge. The loud neighing of the horses was a horrible sound, but the roaring water and the screaming of the terrified children was all the parents could hear.

When Anderson saw the water rushing along, he yelled, "Hang on tight everyone. Hold on to something!" His hands gripped the reins even tighter than before.

Then, out of nowhere appeared an appalling sight. The new bridge built just four years before was overrun with a torrent of water so heavy that waves were dashing against it. Giant tree limbs were crashing into the sides of the bridge with a strength no human could withstand. Already part of the bridge was broken and floating rapidly downstream.

Sensing the hopelessness of the moment, Laura turned toward her children and yelled at the top of her voice, "Hold on to the wagon, and pray!" Her quick turn loosened the Bible and sent it into the churning water. Reaching for the treasured book, Laura lost her balance, fell from the seat and was immediately pulled away by the raging river. Carried downstream, she heard the frantic calls of her children as she struggled to stay afloat.

CHAPTER FOURTEEN

Stunned at the sight of their mother washed away from them by the torrent of water, the children screamed even more loudly. The brave father held tightly to the reins and yelled for Nelle and Opal to hang on to the other three children. As their pleas for their mother subsided, they huddled together, sobbing softly. Laura had been forced out into the turbulent water so quickly that no one could have saved her; yet, they all felt guilty.

Amid the crying, Nelle reached out to her father. "Papa, how can we save her? Where is she? Do you think she is still alive?"

As Anderson caught his breath, he muttered, "Just hang on, Nelle. One thing at a time."

The young girl saw that her father was about to lose control of the reins of the floundering horses, so she knew she must concentrate on her siblings. Even though all were soaked to the skin, no one was complaining about the discomfort. All were too much in shock over their loss.

Before the wagon had come to the end of the long bridge, the raging river had begun to calm itself enough for the horses to move more easily. Anderson had to keep his mind on forcing the family wagon onto land

and finding shelter. He refused to face the horrible truth of his lost mate. That fact would destroy him. As the image of her disappearing body in the angry water kept coming to mind, he would shake his head and stare at the horses.

Slowly the rainstorm waned to a gentle shower, and with their soggy belongings, a sorrowful family began to make their way into the town of Blackburn. Nelle knew not to talk to her father until he was ready. More out of respect than of fear, she had to keep her own sorrow to herself for now.

Finally, Anderson found a stopping place for the wagon. As he turned around, Nelle saw the reddened eyes and grim aspect of her brave father. She motioned to the children to listen.

Before he could speak, little five-year-old Donna begged, "Please, Papa, tell us where Mama went and how we can bring her back!" Then baby Owen and little Daisy started weeping loudly.

The broken-hearted father began. "We are not going to give up. Your mother is a brave woman and not a bad swimmer. These things happen. Somewhere downstream we can hope she found solace and, yes, a rescue. You children can all start praying now. And don't stop."

Just then, Donna, searching in the rubble in the wagon, noticed that the dog was missing. She cried out, "Papa, we must pray for Lucy, too. I can't find her!" Then the crying began again.

In desperation, Anderson knew he must try to find the Barnes family. Just then, he heard the familiar voice of Frank.

"Hey, there. We thought we'd never see you guys again. Looks like your wagon took a beating." As

Frank caught a close look at Anderson's face, he prepared for the bad news.

"Frank, we've lost Laura. She's somewhere downstream."

Not wanting to wait for more news, Jane ran to the wagon and started trying to comfort the children. She attempted to take over for their missing mother and left the men to work out a plan.

Frank took Anderson into town to find the sheriff. The memory of his urging his friend to cross the raging river in the violent storm was causing Frank horrible guilt. For once, he was at a loss for words.

On the town square sat the sheriff's office. Frank took over the details of filing the missing person's report. The sheriff advised them to stay in town for a few days just in case someone found Laura. Anderson wanted a search to start immediately, and he wanted to be part of it. The sheriff assured him they would do all they could and the best thing the husband could do was to stay calm and comfort his family.

Jane and Frank tried to console Anderson with the news that they would stay with the children and help as long as they were needed. He kept pacing back and forth looking at the river. Jane feared that there might easily be a body washed up downstream, but she couldn't dwell on that ending.

She and Nelle brought the children together and tried to keep their thoughts on happier times. They found a park for prairie schooners, and with a campfire, they made a dinner of the food saved for the last meal of the trip. Surely the next morning would bring better news. The children all had Laura in their bedtime prayers. As Jane heard the close of the prayers, she suddenly realized that Anderson had left the park. In her concern for the children, she had ignored an even bigger problem.

CHAPTER FIFTEEN

Laura's attempts to swim were useless against such a strong current. After a few minutes of struggling to stay on top of the water long enough to breathe, she was thrown into an overhanging oak tree. As she struck the tree with a resounding thud, she heard a crack in her left leg.

Her cries from the pain were not heard by anyone upstream as the wind was carrying the sound in the other direction. In spite of her pain, she began to realize she was safely held by the intersection of two strong branches. *At least I won't drown!* she thought.

Out of the immediate danger, she began to panic about the fate of her family. Where were the children? What happened to Anderson? Were they all adrift in the dreadful river? There was no way her five children could have been saved from her same fate. Then she screamed for an hour, partly from pain but primarily for help. But the family couldn't hear her. Finally, fearing she was the only one who survived the tragic storm, she began to sob until she was so exhausted that she fell asleep.

After what must have been several hours, she heard a crying sound, more animal than human. Awakening to the thought that one of her children was stranded in another tree, she heard a barking, faint but strangely familiar. The rain had stopped, and the once frightful Arkansas River now seemed a calmer waterway. Looking at a persimmon tree, she caught sight of her dear little dog. Lucy was cradled in the crotch of two helpful branches also. Now Lucy was crying like a baby as she recognized the voice of her Laura.

The dog, unharmed by the watery experience, stretched her legs and scampered out of her tree cradle and down to a bed of soggy leaves. Then she ran to the next tree and climbed to be near Laura. The little beagle snuggled as close as she could be and added warmth to her shivering owner.

"Well, look who came to give me hope. I can't give up now," whispered Laura. Still groggy from her exhaustion, Laura drifted off into a dreamy state, kept warm by the loving dog.

Not long after, a local farmer paddled by in his fishing boat. Seeing a dark-haired stranger approach, the beagle began barking loudly. The man, startled to be barked at by a dog in a tree, looked up to see an even stranger sight.

"Well, ma'am. Pardon me, but could you use some help?"

Laura cried out, "Oh, yes. Please. I am lost, and I think my leg is broken." Then, overcome with emotion, she started crying and couldn't tell him anymore.

The stranger secured his rowboat and started toward Laura's tree. He said, "My name is Jeff Fulton. I live here in the country outside of Blackburn, and I'll try to get you to a doctor as soon as I can."

Laura tried to get herself out of the tree, but she was in too much pain to help. All she could do was cry. Fulton assured her he could carry her to the rowboat.

First, he took an extra oar to keep her leg straight and tore his outer shirt to secure the leg to the oar. Lucy sensed that this stranger was not to be feared, and she stopped her barking.

After all three were safe in the boat, Laura was able to talk. She explained, "My family was crossing the river in our wagon, and the flash flood came so quickly! I was swept overboard and...." The emotion overtook her. She couldn't talk about what might have happened to the others.

Fulton calmed her by saying, "I understand. Don't try to talk. We'll hope for the best. Just trust me."

With two more miles to go, Fulton felt the need to help her by carrying the conversation. As he gently plied the oars, he said, "I spend a lot of days out here on this part of the river, so you don't need to be afraid. We'll have a safe, short trip to the next clearing. I farm out here on weekends and work in Pawnee for a lawyer through the week. That way I never get bored." He guided the rowboat upstream to a spot near the bridge.

"My cabin is just around the bend here. I can carry you there where you can rest. Then I'll go for a doctor and notify the sheriff to see about your family." As Fulton talked, Lucy came to his side for a comforting tummy rub.

Fulton carried Laura carefully from his boat to the cabin, keeping her leg steady on the oar. He thought about what this fishing trip had produced. Glad that he could save this woman's life, he still wondered what he would discover about the fate of her family in the ensuing hours.

CHAPTER SIXTEEN

When Anderson left the others at the park, he ran back to the river's edge. Scanning the scene, he looked for signs of Laura. After five minutes of walking along a neglected and slippery footpath, he found a scrap of her flowered shawl festooned in a blackjack tree. The shawl was his last glimpse of Laura as she had disappeared into the frightful water. He grasped at the scrap of remembrance and asked himself, "Why wasn't she able to be held by one of us? Why was she the one without a helper? Why couldn't I grab her and hold the horses? She told the rest of us to hold on."

Two minutes later, he stumbled over the remnants of her crushed sewing box on a pile of rocks. As he kept on with his fruitless search, he found a crumpled book with a black cover. It was just the last chapter of something. As he picked up the dripping pages, he realized it was the family Bible, and only the part called Revelation. He remembered how Laura was protecting that precious book before she was swept over the side of the wagon. At that moment, he knew he must return to shelter the family.

As Anderson turned to go back to the family, Frank Barnes came running to him, saying, "What did you find?"

"Just her shawl and some other household relics on the shore, and this." He handed the last chapter of the Bible to Frank. His friend's heart sank as he thought of the symbolism of the word "revelation."

The bedraggled father didn't want to talk, and Frank sensed his agony. Finally, Anderson mumbled to himself, "I don't see how Laura could have survived, but I can't tell that to the children."

"No, of course not. And you must stop thinking that way. Look, you just need to rest here with the family for a while. That horrible time on the bridge has taken its toll on all of you. Jane is brewing some coffee near our wagon. Help yourself."

"Frank, I must keep on searching. I know that the sheriff said he would get to work on finding her, but he doesn't understand. My Laura is out there somewhere!"

Meanwhile, back in Blackburn, as Jane tried to answer the questions of the four children, she was devising her own plan for help. She had seen the young mother swept from the wagon, fighting against the current. Even a strong swimmer could not survive those conditions, and she feared that Laura was not a good swimmer. Was there any way she and Frank could rear these children? But what about Anderson? He wouldn't want to give up his family. Maybe when they all got settled in Pawnee, there would be a nice single woman whom Anderson would meet or perhaps there would be a young widow and…. No, that's not right. Laura must be out there somewhere. Surely she must still be alive.

Someone else was having somber thoughts about the future. Nelle had given up hope that she would ever see her mother again. She had grabbed for Laura as the water swept her away, but all she caught was a scrap of her blue gingham dress. As she closed her eyes, Nelle could still see her mother's body being pulled by the ugly river current.

Being the eldest of five children, Nelle had assumed more duties of child rearing than any sibling should. Now at the age of nine, she looked into the future months. She knew that more burdens would fall on her. Other little girls might play with dolls, but Nelle had her own siblings for dolls. She loved her sisters and brother but feared the work ahead of her. Papa was not afraid of toiling in the field, but he had always expected Mama to do the woman's work, no matter how tired she was.

Suddenly, Nelle was sobbing quietly so as not to alarm the others. *No more Mother. Never to see her again. No talk. No hugs. No laughter.* She pulled her little sunbonnet over her face and remembered seeing her mother do the same on the first day of the journey.

CHAPTER SEVENTEEN

Awakening to unbearable pain, Laura found herself in a strange bed in a cabin she had never seen. Then she realized that she must have passed out as she was carried from the boat to this lonely place. When she called out for help, no one answered. Terrified, she began to cry, and immediately, as if in answer to a call for help, the little beagle jumped into her arms and began licking her face. Laura was so relieved to see her furry friend that she laughed in spite of her pain and fear.

She noticed that there was a note by the bed. The nice farmer had written in very clear handwriting the following: "Ma'am. I knew you would be frightened to find yourself alone, but you need medical help right now. I have left you in the care of your sweet dog. I am returning quickly with the town doctor. He needs to set your leg and give you some sedative. Try to be calm. Your friend, Jeff Fulton. P.S. Help yourself to the cold chicken leg and fresh apple on the table. Don't forget to drink the water." Before Laura could finish her food, she heard the calming voice of her new friend. He had brought a doctor.

"Laura, this man is going to make you feel a lot better," promised Fulton as he helped Dr. Connors get his equipment set up. "I explained to the doctor how you escaped from the river, and he is prepared to get you ready to travel very soon."

The doctor explained, "First, I need to give you some sedative for the pain you are feeling now and for the pain you will feel as I set your leg. It is going to take some manipulation, so you need to be very brave."

Laura swallowed some pills and began to feel very woozy. She soon was dreaming of camping beside a lovely river with her family and enjoying a picnic lunch. As she dreamed, the doctor told Fulton that for her trip back to Blackburn, she would need to be sedated but not to this extent. He suggested liquor to deaden the pain but not to knock her out. She needed to be able to cooperate with her husband as he drove her in their wagon to be sure that her leg set properly. As he tried to set the bones back in place, he discovered that there was a shattering of some of the bone material. Some ligaments were damaged and a tendon was broken. After several minutes of work, Dr. Connors realized that the left leg would be shorter than the other. She would need to have a special shoe built up or she would always hobble.

While Laura was on her dream picnic and recovering from the first-aid house call of the doctor, news was traveling around Blackburn. The sheriff had learned from the doctor's wife that Jeff Fulton had a wounded woman at his cabin. She was in her late twenties and had light-brown hair. Rumor had it that she had almost drowned and would never have been found if it hadn't been for a beagle in a tree. Without having the name of the almost-drowned woman, the sheriff felt he had enough evidence to notify the grieving man that his wife had been found.

Just as Anderson and Frank walked into the sheriff's office to once again ask for help, the sheriff told the complicated story of a wounded woman. Anderson knew immediately that the woman and the dog could only belong to him. After getting a hastily drawn map, he thanked the sheriff and started off on foot to rescue his wife.

Frank Barnes grabbed Anderson's arm and said, "Your wagon's still a mess from the flood, and ours is fairly dry. We can make a soft, cushiony ride for Laura with our down comforter. We'll follow this trail and be there in no time."

Arriving at Jeff's cabin, Anderson and Frank were greeted by the tall, handsome man who had saved Laura's life. The husband expressed his thanks to Jeff and was hearing the details of the rescue when the doctor appeared at the door to say he had finished the cast on Laura's leg.

Anderson was led inside to see his wife. He had never seen her looking so small and helpless as she did lying in that strange bed, and he saw a new beauty in her.

"I thought I'd never see you again, Laura. The children and I have missed you so much."

"Please tell me they are all still alive," she begged.

Before he could do more than nod his answer, a wet nose rubbed his hand.

"Oh, girl, you are a welcome sight to see, too," he laughed as he grabbed the playful dog and held her and Laura close to his chest.

Then Anderson noticed the doctor motioning to him to step outside. He walked out onto the porch.

The doctor said, "I think you should know that this procedure wasn't perfect. When your wife broke her leg, she must have hit that tree with a powerful impact. Part of the bone shattered. I set it as best I could, but with a piece missing, the left leg is now shorter than before. She will always walk with an uneven gait. Perhaps you can whittle a wooden heel for that one shoe to help her along. I'm sorry. She will need a crutch, of course. Perhaps the crutch will only be temporary."

This blow was softened by the fact that his dear wife was found alive and was being restored to her family. Anderson would tell Laura this news at a later time. He thanked the doctor; then suddenly he realized there was no way he could pay him.

Dr. Connors, sensing the embarrassment, said, "Oh, and don't try to pay for this. Someone has already taken care of that. I was glad to be part of the adventure. I plan to tell this story to my grandchildren. So long."

Lying on soft blankets, Laura was placed in the Barnes wagon by Anderson and Frank. As the sun began to set, Laura was regaining consciousness. Eager to get back to her children, she promised all three men that she was ready for the trip to Blackburn. Fulton helped the men to steady her for the journey. He even added a quilt to cushion her ride.

As she waved goodbye to her new friend, she noticed that he had handed her husband a bottle of Scotch. After a few miles, she asked Anderson what he was thinking. "You know we have never been a drinking family. That is one of our rules."

Anderson said, "Very soon you may see that this is the only medicine that will get you down the road."

Sure enough, within two miles, all of the heavy sedative had worn off, and Laura was ready for anything to relieve the pain. Anderson didn't even mind that her talk seemed to make no sense. At least she was not feeling the pain of the bumpy road.

"Anderson, I thought I'd never see you again. You and the children were so far away, and all I had was Lucy, bless her heart. Are the little ones all right? I couldn't even hear you as I called back to the bridge for help. I thought you all had drowned. How could I be so lucky? Don't ever let me cross a river again! Promise? Am I talking too much? Lucy saved my life. Did you meet that Jeff Fulton? He is a real friend of ours. We should have him over sometime. He gave me this quilt. I just love it. I think I'm doing all the talking. I'll stop now."

Frank turned to Anderson and reassured him that the children would all be bedded down in the Barnes' wagon. By morning the "sedative" would have worn off, and Laura would be back to her normal self to greet her children. What happened to the rest of the "sedative" that night remained a secret, but the bottle was never seen again.

CHAPTER EIGHTEEN

The next morning Laura was awakened by little Daisy. The four-year-old had burrowed out of her wagon and run over to the Barnes' wagon. Jane Barnes had alerted the children the night before that their mother would be returning, but she must be treated carefully because of her wounded leg.

Daisy crept softly up to the side of the wagon and whispered, "Mama, are you in there? I want a hug."

As Laura looked out, she saw the red-haired child trying to climb up into the bedding. She reached down to help her. The two were reunited with Daisy giggling in delight.

Soon all her siblings had joined her with Jane watching over them. Anderson had been up since dawn, working on a crutch that he had carved out of a post oak branch. It was the perfect size for Laura, and she was so pleased.

Frank appeared in the midst of the crowd and announced that he had prepared a breakfast for their last morning on the road. All joined in the fun of some burnt bacon and bread with coffee for the grownups. Within twenty minutes, the travelers had cleaned up their campsite and started on their way to the new land of Pawnee.

Frank and Anderson shared the wagon seat for the last part of the trip to do some last-minute planning.

Frank asked, "Do you think this short trip will be too painful for Laura?"

"She can stand it. The joy of being back with all of us will keep her going. You weren't thinking she might need some sedative, were you?" laughed Anderson.

"Too bad if she does. I remember where we poured it out last night," chuckled Frank, as he took out his wrinkled map. "This paper shows we'll pass right through town on our way to the farmland."

"At least we'll be finding a trail that won't have the undergrowth of the Cross Timbers. Those last few miles of heavy briars really played havoc with the horses," said Anderson. "Say, when will we be meeting up with our Indian landlord?"

Frank assured him he should not be concerned about the land deal. "I wouldn't be surprised if White Eagle will be there when we arrive. He has his eyes out for us."

The two wagons pulled around a small hillside, and suddenly there was the main street with a town square and stores surrounding it.

Laura and Jane were amazed at the possibilities. "Look, Jane, there is a funeral home and furniture store all in one. And look at that mercantile store beside it."

"Maybe soon we can come to town and get better acquainted with Pawnee," suggested Jane. "Right now we have three more miles to go to find home."

Just beyond the town square on a weathered sycamore tree was a wanted poster. The two men paused to read the details.

"Well, Frank, it looks like another gang is at work in Pawnee. They have held up the bank again. We'll have to guard our gold watches!"

"Sure thing, Anderson. Soon as I find one, I'll guard it."

A mile farther they crossed Black Bear Creek. Across the bridge was a roadside stand with a farmer selling homemade ice cream. The sign read, "Free ice cream to travelers."

"Is this a mirage or what?" laughed Frank.

"Well", said Anderson, "just in case it's for real, let's see if we can prove we've been traveling."

The old farmer yelled out from the stand, "I have proof by the red Pawnee dirt on your covered wagon. Come set a spell."

As he saw all the children jump from the wagons, the farmer called to his wife, "Mildred, we're doin' a land-office business right now. Better bring some more ice cream."

It was a welcome treat and well deserved as the newcomers met Sam Parsons, the retired mayor and now a gentleman farmer. After the men explained why they had come to Pawnee, Parsons assured them that White Eagle was a reliable Indian landlord who would treat them fairly.

Just then a horseman rode up, held out his hand to Frank and said, "I'm John White Eagle. I believe you must be Frank Barnes. I heard you had arrived. And would this be Anderson Mansfield with you?"

As the men shook hands, their new landlord told them he'd lead them down the road to their new homestead. Inside the wagons, the children were fearful and beginning to cry as they saw the arrival of the Indian. The mothers reassured them but were trying to calm themselves also.

White Eagle waited as the weary travelers readied themselves for the final few miles. Farmer Parsons, seeing the worried look on Nelle's face, said, "You'll be finding new friends at the Oak Grove schoolhouse. My little granddaughter Beth just loves that school. Who knows? She might even be your best friend. She is nine years old as of last week. Isn't that about your age?" Nelle nodded. Smiling at the thought of a new friend, Nelle climbed back in the wagon that began to follow the Indian and his pinto pony northward along the dusty trail.

The children's excitement over the day had been calmed by the delicious ice cream. Now the repetitive thumping of the wooden wagon wheels was lulling the youngsters into an afternoon nap. Even Nelle was caught in a confused dream that reviewed the past few days.

"Look out! The Dalton guys are coming!" She looked up the main street to see five masked men on horses fleeing what must have been a bank robbery. Shots rang out as two men fell dead in the dirt outside the mercantile store. One woman was sobbing while two others ran for help. Blood ran along the unpaved road.

Just then, the kind old farmer, Mr. Parsons, sauntered down the street and said, "Well, look who's here! Nelle, would you like some strawberry ice cream? I'll bet you just got out of school."

Before she could answer, she saw White Eagle in his Pawnee Indian clothes, aiming a bow and arrow at a little boy who had skipped school. "Stop, boy. We don't allow truancy at Oak Grove School!"

"No, don't shoot that little boy!" cried Nelle.

Laura shook her sleeping daughter, then held her closely as Nelle came out of her dream.

"Mama! The Indian was about to shoot some poor little boy, and the Daltons were robbing the bank and killing people on the main street, and Mr. Parsons didn't even care, he just...."

"Nelle. It's O.K. You were having a really bad nightmare." She wiped Nelle's tears and hugged her back to reality. "We're just about to get to the farmland. You'll want to be awake for this."

Opal, Donna, Daisy and Owen had awakened at Nelle's crying and were already poised to see the new homestead.

What they saw was a forty-acre field, just ready to be worked. What White Eagle had not revealed was that another family had tried to make a life on that very spot with tenant farming, but they had failed. The young husband brought his new bride down from Kansas to the territory with big dreams. She pictured a cottage with a climbing yellow rose around the door. He saw himself tilling the fertile soil and raising fine crops. Soon a family of at least three sons would be able to help him become a prosperous farmer who could buy the land. What he found was tough soil, unreliable rainfall, and a wheat crop that failed.

As the winter crept in, his beautiful wife became ill with typhoid from contaminated creek water. Living in their temporary dugout, she was unable to stay warm enough in the bitterly cold weather. By February, she had died, along with their stillborn child. After the burial of his wife and son in the town cemetery just east of the farm, the broken-hearted young husband returned to Kansas. That was two years ago. The dugout home, once strong enough to withstand one harsh winter, had gradually disintegrated into an ugly mound of red Pawnee dirt at the edge of the lease, a puzzle to newcomers.

Anderson and Frank dismounted first and began discussing the business of their leases with White Eagle. The terms were agreeable, with the landlord taking his percentage of the profits from the first crops for payment. Laura and Jane planned the immediate work of housing for the first night.

"You know that the men will have to start digging our family dugout tomorrow," said Laura, "but for a while we'll be sleeping in the wagons."

"Frank keeps telling me that the dugout is a temporary home. Otherwise, I couldn't live with the thought of that awful place."

"I think we'll be thankful," said Laura, "that we have that awful place when the cold winter comes and we are cozy inside."

Smiling, Jane said, "Laura, at the first of this trip, I was afraid you were not brave and strong enough to endure. But I've seen a new woman emerge who can survive a raging river, a broken leg, and a future in a dugout. I guess this is what pioneers are called to do."

As the sun set over their new farmland, both families happily bedded down again in their own covered wagons unaware that others had toiled on that very land with nothing to show for it but a small well-covered mound and two lonely graves up on the hill east of town.

CHAPTER NINETEEN

Late April in Pawnee County had the promise of perfect weather. The storms that had almost destroyed the newcomers' entrance back at Blackburn had left the soil pliable and ready for planting. Filled with anticipation and a sense of urgency, Anderson knew he must get the land ready for crops for his family's survival that first year.

Yet, the task of constructing a temporary home took precedence. Anderson and Frank had been fearful of the fate of a dugout after remembering tales of previous settlers with water-soaked belongings. Now was the time for decision. They both opted for a soddy.

Anderson's goal was to finish the house in one week. Then, with the sod removed, the ground would be easier to plow for the first seeds. As he stepped down from the covered wagon to prepare for the first day of heavy labor, his mind was on the exact crop and the additional list of vegetables for the family's survival. He was so preoccupied that he didn't even see Frank Barnes riding across the open country.

"Hey, neighbor," called Barnes. "Have I got some good news for you!"

"Well, I could use some. The best news would be that you have come to start digging sod," suggested Anderson.

"Better than that. I just rented a machine for both of us. It's a plow that digs sod. Forget that shovel. This thing will dig it, and then we cut it to fit our needs."

At a loss for words, Anderson sat on the ground to take in the possibilities.

"But, wait. The real news is that three guys at the mercantile store heard about our plans, and they are coming over this morning to help us. They say that with the sod-digging machine they can probably finish up in two days. I'll be part of the crew; so with you, that will be five good men on the job. It's kind of like a barn raising."

Anderson jumped to his feet and said, "Nobody's this lucky, especially me. Just be honest with me, Barnes. What is this going to cost us? You know we can't hire this work done. A fancy rental tool, three guys working two days. Whoever heard of such a thing!"

Barnes shrugged his shoulders and admitted, "You're too smart for me. I can't fool you, can I? The payback comes the next time another guy comes to town and starts to build his soddy. Our names will be at the top of the list. Can you pay that kind of bill?"

Sighing, Anderson said, "It sounds pretty good when you put it that way. But you've still rented an expensive sod-cutter tool. How do you think we can afford that?"

"Well, to set your mind at ease, I didn't really rent it," admitted Barnes.

"You mean you stole it?"

"Of course not. It belongs to my Uncle Travis. I am just borrowing it, and so are you."

By this time, Laura and the children had found their way to the fireside and started breakfast. Anderson shared the happy story of friendly town folk helping them, and Laura was overjoyed. She felt tears forming, but there was no need to hide them from Anderson this time. These were tears of delight at finding her new town would be a real home for them. She had imagined herself digging sod and laying the squares along with her husband. Now she could tend to the children and keep the men fed. The pain from her recent accident was a constant reminder of her limited ability, but she had already devised a way to cook from a sitting position. With her able-bodied older daughters, Laura was sure she could keep the workers fed.

Within an hour, the three strong-looking men arrived on horseback, pulling a strange sod cutter and looking eager for their task. "Sorry it took us so long," said the tallest of the three. "This machine just doesn't want to go as fast as the horses do." Then they dismounted, tied their horses to a cottonwood tree and headed toward the designated section of buffalo grass for sod removal.

Laura was amazed at the organized work of digging the sod in such a uniform way. Each cut was at the same depth as the previous one. The buffalo grass with its thickly-packed roots was going to make fine bricks for their new home. She was tempted to join the crew of men just to make sure of some special details she wanted to have in her new home.

Anderson saw her coming toward them. The newly-hewn crutch had slowed her down, but he was proud of her for her effort to keep trying. He met her with a suggestion. "Laura, the best way you can help us today is to make sure the children stay away from the work

87

area. Also, we'll have hungry men at noon. I know you'll be ready for them."

Laura smiled and withdrew, knowing that Anderson's plans for a 12 x 14 house with one door were already being discussed. Her hope of at least one window would depend on several things, mainly the cost. The glass would be expensive, and as the weight of the roof could cause the sod bricks to sink, the glass might crack. She knew the arguments against her ideas. In her mind she pictured some nail kegs for chairs and a fireplace at the far end. She wished she could make sure they would leave a hole for the smoke to leave the room. She felt her arguments for the fireplace would have to win out. They had to cook food and they had to keep warm. An outside fireplace would really be difficult for wintertime cooking.

Laura was terrified but thankful that Mildred Parsons had dropped by last week with a surprise gift of burlap sacks. The dear woman said these should be sewn together to cover their ceiling. That was a sure way to keep snakes and spiders from falling into their new homes.

With all the trouble of living in a sod house, at least it would be better than a dugout. She had heard of settlers who found themselves bailing out water when heavy rains flooded their dugout. Others had warned that digging into the soil for a house opened prairie dog holes and remaining fleas would be a problem later, especially during the rainy season.

Suddenly she saw that the children needed to be entertained. By this time, the Barnes family had come to help and to visit. Laura and Jane found that seven children were ready for a game of fox and geese. Little beagle Lucy was delighted to run around and join the fun. This scene would repeat itself at the Barnes' farm place as soon as this first soddy was in place.

CHAPTER TWENTY

As Laura and Jane took a break from sod house building, they joined their children in a game of hide and seek. After a short while, they sat beneath a large oak tree and began talking about the local school. Soon, out of nowhere, a beautiful young woman on a brown horse rode toward them and stopped.

As she dismounted, she introduced herself. "Pardon me, ladies. I would like to welcome you to Pawnee. I am Gertrude Wheeler, the schoolteacher at Oak Grove School."

Jane hurriedly brushed the dust from a tree stump next to her and, offering the teacher a seat, said, "Please join us here in the shade. I am Jane Barnes, and this is my neighbor and best friend, Laura Mansfield."

The young woman replied, "I am so glad to meet our newest citizens of Pawnee County, and I want to get acquainted with your children also. You see, you are in our district for the Oak Grove School. I serve as the teacher in our one-room schoolhouse. It covers the first through eighth grades. When they finish that course, they are ready for the Pawnee High School in town."

Laura responded, "We were afraid we had arrived too late in the school year for our children to be admitted."

Before she had finished her sentence, the seven children had made their way over to their mothers and were nervously waiting for the proper moment to speak to the newcomer.

"Oh, you have come at a perfect time. We have six more weeks of school, and in that time, they can get acquainted with the students and our way of learning. I'd like to meet these fine young folks who are hiding behind you," smiled the attractive auburn-haired teacher.

Jane arranged the children in order of age and began. "Now first we have the Mansfields: Owen, Daisy, Donna, Opal and Nelle. These last two are seven and nine years old. Then my children, from the Barnes family, are Fred and Hazel. They also are seven and nine years old."

After a sharp bark, she added, "Oh, yes, and that little dog by Fred is Lucy; she is a Mansfield."

Shaking hands with each of the children and patting the head of one dog, Miss Wheeler noticed a sense of fear in the three small ones; but the four school age children looked eager and pleasantly excited.

Returning to the mothers, she suggested, "Ladies, I'd like to invite Opal, Nelle, Hazel and Fred to join us at school tomorrow. We'll wait until later for Owen, Daisy, Donna and is it Lucy? In a few years, the younger ones will be old enough, and, who knows? Maybe we can even start some dog training. Please join us tomorrow. Let's try this idea. Have them arrive after lunchtime. I'll prepare the other students for their arrival during our morning classes, and your children can experience the afternoon classes."

As she explained the plan, she watched the smiles appear and the eyes get wider with anticipation.

"Oh, can we do that, Mama, please?" begged Nelle.

"I really must ask Papa, but I will try my best to let you go," she responded.

"That's settled then," said Miss Wheeler. "It's been a real pleasure to meet all of you, and we'll hope to see you tomorrow."

Then she mounted her horse and took off down the road. All seven children were waving goodbye until she disappeared in a cloud of dust.

Opal suddenly asked, "What will we wear? Our overalls won't do for school time!"

Nelle reminded her that each of the Mansfield sisters had a dress and they would look just fine. Hazel Barnes couldn't decide between her red dress or her flowery apron dress with the lace trim. As she explained the advantages and disadvantages of each, Fred Barnes walked away, secure in the belief that his overalls would suit him for a day at school.

While the children planned their first-day wardrobe, Laura and Jane told the fathers about their visit from the schoolteacher. At first, the men, tired from the day full of sod house building, were annoyed by any interruption.

Then Barnes slapped his knee and said, "Hold on, now! We are talking about our children's future here. You bet those four kids can go over to the schoolhouse tomorrow."

Anderson interrupted with, "How are we going to get them there? We can't just send them down an unknown road by themselves. We're still trying to put a roof over our heads!"

Barnes replied, "Here's what we'll do. Jane can drive the wagon. Isn't that school about two miles from here? I guess we could spare her from slapping mud against sod for one hour. They can find their way home on foot, and Jane will be back here to return to her sod work. My wife is a good one to look over the school and bring us a reliable report. I think our four kids will be in good hands with her, don't you?"

Feeling ashamed of his immediate antagonism, Anderson answered, "Of course. I was letting the present moment get in the way of the future!"

Even at a distance, the children heard the two mothers cheering and clapping, and they knew that the good news was they would be in school tomorrow.

CHAPTER TWENTY-ONE

The schoolroom was buzzing with conversations when the four new students arrived. Lunchtime was over, and the schoolteacher was busy outside talking to Jane Barnes. Nelle and Opal found an empty two-seater desk and slipped into place. Fred and Hazel found an empty desk right by an open window. When the teacher entered the room, she was delighted to see the new children.

"Boys and girls, I want you to meet our newest students, the Mansfield girls, Nelle and Opal, and Hazel and Fred Barnes. By the end of the day, we want to make them feel at home here. Beth Parsons, you can be the Mansfields' helper and special friend, and Jude Comstock, you take care of Hazel and Fred."

Nelle looked across the aisle and saw a smiling blonde-haired girl coming toward her with a textbook.

Miss Wheeler explained, "Both of you sisters can share this book. It is yours for the classroom and to take home. We'll start you both with the First Reader."

As the teacher walked to her desk, Nelle looked at the stories in the new book and knew she should be in a more advanced level, but now was not the time to complain.

When recess came, the children quickly walked to the grassy area and found their favorite play areas. Several boys were playing catch, and a dozen children started a game of red rover. Beth Parsons helped Nelle and Opal join her in a game of jacks.

Nelle asked, "Do you have a grandfather who treats newcomers to ice cream?"

Beth laughed and said, "Of course. Now I remember he told me to watch for a new girl at Oak Grove who was just my age, and that's you! I think we'll be the best of friends."

Seeing a sad look on Opal's face, Beth added, "Opal, you are going to be my best little friend."

Beth showed special skill at the jacks game as she tossed the little red ball quickly, scooping up the shiny jacks before the ball bounced. Opal wished she could have a try at the game, and Beth noticed her interest.

"Here, Opal. You see if you can do the pigs in a basket trick. It's not so hard."

Opal was thrilled to be included in the fun. As she tossed the pretty ball, though, it took a turn to the left and then knocked into the jacks.

Beth laughed kindly and said, "All you need is some practice. By tomorrow you'll be better than I am. Here, take my little pouch of jacks home. I've got another. You can have it for keeps."

Opal smiled at her new friend and thanked her several times. Beth carefully placed the jacks and ball in a soft white bag with a pull tie. Then she handed the pouch to Opal.

"If you lose this bag or if it gets torn, don't worry. I get these from my grandpa. He smokes a pipe and his pipe tobacco comes in these. Oh, there's the bell. Miss Wheeler always calls us back in that way after recess, and we have to be quick! She takes off points for lateness."

Three happy girls ran to the school door and took their seats. Nelle noticed some strange lines on the chalkboard that the school teacher had prepared during recess. It was time for the older students' lesson which looked like some kind of word puzzle.

A twelve-year-old boy was called to the front, and he began to fill in a sentence on what looked like a roadmap going west to east. Nelle was curious about what was happening and thankful she was not the student at the board. Even though her class was supposed to be studying in the First Reader, she was intrigued with the strange terms and precise placement of a sentence on a roadmap that was gradually becoming a tree as it moved farther east.

Suddenly she heard the teacher's ruler tapping on her desk, and she learned quickly that the First Reader students were not to be distracted by the advanced students' lesson. So she returned to page 23 in the First Reader and copied, "The pen and ink are on the stand" on her slate. Her one-room schoolhouse lesson that day was to mind her own business.

At the close of the school day, Miss Wheeler handed each new student a list of necessary supplies. She reminded them that tomorrow would be a full day for them and they needed to arrive by 8:30 a.m. The two-mile walk home gave the new students a chance to compare notes. Hazel told of a new friend she met at recess, and Fred told about Jude Comstock.

"Jude didn't know how to talk to a girl, so Hazel just had to wander off and meet up with the jump rope girls. Then Jude was a little more fun. We went off to play catch. He's pretty good at that."

"Well," said Hazel. "I had a lot of fun at jump rope, and the girls treated me all right. But one girl was especially nice. She told me she liked my dress. I'm sure glad I decided on the flowery apron one with the lace on the edge. Then she offered to let me sit at her desk after recess. I didn't know what the slate exercise was, so she helped me with that."

Nelle asked, "What about this First Reader, Hazel? We're both nine years old, and I think that book is just too easy for us. Did you look at the end of the book? It still has little kid stuff like, 'One day, this old hen took her chickens down to a small brook.' I'm ready for something harder than that. I'd like to learn things like those road map sentences the big children did today."

Hazel thought a minute and said, "Nelle, I'm not in any hurry, but you could tell the teacher about it. At least we didn't get stuck with the Primer."

"I plan to ask her to move me up tomorrow. At our break time, I sneaked into the bookcase and checked on the Sixth Reader."

"Don't tell me you want to jump into that one," laughed Hazel.

"No way. I just wanted to see what's ahead for us, and guess what I found?"

Before Hazel could answer, Nelle answered her own question. "Remember how my mama loves poetry. Well, that Sixth Reader is just full of her kind of reading. There's Wordsworth and lots of Shakespeare, too. I think we're going to learn a lot here."

Close behind them, Opal and Fred were enjoying the walk. In her hand, Opal felt the soft tobacco pouch with her new game inside. She held it close to her face. It had an unusual smell. Opal had never known her grandfathers, but she sensed that the tobacco pouch must be the smell of grandpas. That would probably go away after a few days, she thought. Happy over the day, she hummed as she walked along. Fred was kicking a stone until it took a wrong turn into a dense weed patch.

Finally, the four children heard the sound of their fathers' voices as they worked at applying a layer of sod to the roof on their new home. Each child had a story to share about the new life at school, but Opal was the only one with a tobacco pouch.

CHAPTER TWENTY-TWO

Within a week, two new homes appeared on the "west half of the northeast Quarter of Section twenty-five in Township twenty-two, north of range four, east of the Indian Meridian, containing 80 acres, more or less, according to the government survey" in Pawnee County, Oklahoma Territory. The description was more dignified and permanent than the two houses.

That legal language would remain long after the two soddies had crumbled back into their own sod bed. However, these homes would serve their purpose for at least one year.

In that same week, much had been accomplished two miles west of the homes. Nelle had learned that the tree-house designs on the chalkboard were really a new phase of American education called diagramming sentences. This method was destined to explain the purpose of the parts of speech and to make grammar teaching more feasible to students. Opal acquired a remarkable skill at the game of jacks and met new friends who appreciated her ability. After careful testing, Hazel and Nelle both advanced to McGuffey's Second Reader, much to the relief of Nelle. Fred Barnes tolerated the classwork but excelled at recess. He was always cheered on at the game of red rover.

Fred's new friend and desk partner, Jude, however, had turned out to be a troublemaker in the classroom. What appeared to be an unfriendliness at first had developed into a surly attitude toward school and toward the other students. He even wanted to argue with the teacher over one of his late assignments.

Walking home from school one afternoon, Nelle noticed that Fred was even more quiet than usual.

She asked, "Fred, what's wrong? You haven't said anything since we left the schoolhouse."

"Oh," he responded. "I'm just kinda fed up with that Jude guy."

"I think he's an old sourpuss," said Hazel. "That first day when we were assigned to him, I thought he was shy, but now I think he's just a mopey boy."

"Well," added Opal, "I heard that he's really older than we are, and that he's not too smart."

"O.K., now that's enough," said Nelle. "Can't anyone find anything good about him? We've only known him for a week, and we need to give him another chance. Fred, you might be his only friend in the whole school. You just need to try harder. Why not think of something nice you can say to him tomorrow?"

"Well, you don't have to sit at the same desk and share supplies with him," replied Fred. "He doesn't even want a friend, I'll bet! Today he just sat there and groaned to himself. Do you know how annoying that can be?" Then, kicking stones along the dusty road, he slipped back into his quiet mood.

Opal broke the silence with, "Maybe Mama could bake cookies and you could take him a few for a surprise."

Fred let her know how impossible that would be by ignoring her suggestion.

Next day at school, Miss Wheeler called the roll, and when she came to Jude's name, there was no answer. She paused, then sat at the front edge of her desk and had a very sad look on her face.

"I want you students to know that Jude Comstock is quite ill. You might have noticed yesterday he was out of sorts and, well, he was downright rude."

A chortle was heard in the back of the room as Dave Barnum muttered, "Jude was rude." Two girls giggled, then stopped abruptly, seeing the look on the schoolteacher's face.

"I don't know the nature of Jude's illness," continued the school teacher. "It could be any number of things. But he is in much pain, and Doctor Small is looking after him. I'd like each of you to take a page from your tablet and, using your very best penmanship, write Jude a note of encouragement. I'll deliver them to his house right after school."

Oak Grove Schoolhouse, District 66, was as quiet as could be as all twenty students wrote their best thoughts to a fellow student. Fred Barnes tried unusually hard to say a kind word, and wrote, "You have very nice hair." Fred was feeling guilty over his harsh words the day before. As Miss Wheeler heard the scratching of the dipped pens, she prayed that those notes would arrive in time. What she had not told the children was the hopelessness of Jude's case. He had a ruptured appendix, and the doctor was not called to the house soon enough. It was too late to operate. What Miss Wheeler did not know was at that very moment the toxic fluids had spread throughout Jude's body, and he was dead before the students finished their notes of encouragement.

Jude's death was the first brush with the end of life for most of the students. Several had suffered the loss of a pet, three remembered the death of grandparents, and one boy had a baby brother who died. Yet, having a fellow classmate die, one who was sitting with them the day before, brought many questions to the children.

Word of his death spread rapidly in the small community before sunset. Nelle and Hazel heard the tragic news from their parents. The schoolteacher did her best to inform the school families of the loss and to announce the cancelling of class for two days.

The next morning, before their chores, Nelle and Hazel began to ask each other the obvious questions. Are children supposed to die? Isn't that just for old people? Are we going to catch his disease? Did he die because we weren't nice enough to him? Where do people go when they die? Is Jude there now? Can he hear us talking about him? Why do they have to bury him?

Laura saw the two girls outside the soddy and knew it was time for them to get busy.

She quickly interrupted their conversation with, "Nelle, you and Hazel would be a big help to Papa if you would put your hands to work on the corn planting. Here, take this sack of kernels and join him at the end of that row." She pointed to the far end of a long row that basked in the warm April sunshine.

Since the Mansfield family had dealt with the questions the previous evening, Laura had nothing else to add. Now was the time to let hard work take over. Soon the two youngsters were following a planting pattern with little time for deep questions.

The following day, the Baptist church of Pawnee held services for Jude. Laura drove the wagon into town with Nelle, Opal, Hazel and Fred. Jane Barnes tended the younger Mansfields. Several of the other Oak Grove students attended along with their schoolteacher, who gave a short but comforting eulogy at the close of the service.

After the closing prayer, as the pine coffin was carried out of the church, Nelle heard a shriek and looked up to see Jude's mother falling in the aisle.

"What's happening, Mama?" she asked.

Before Laura could answer, a woman wailed, "She's fainted from grief."

"Someone get a stretcher for her!" shouted another woman.

The pastor's wife, used to the effects of grief, calmed the ladies and took out smelling salts from behind the pulpit. She cradled the mother's head in her lap and held the salts to her nose.

"Look. She's coming around," said Laura to the children beside her. Patting Nelle's hand, she said, "We mustn't bother her. It's going to be all right."

By this time several women were sobbing, many children joined them in their own crying, and the lonely pine coffin was loaded onto a black wagon. Most of the mourners returned home and left the trip to the cemetery to the family. However, Laura agreed to take her four passengers to the graveside. The trip to the cemetery east of Pawnee took thirty minutes. Now the children had many new questions, and Laura did her best. Finally, a stillness settled over the wagon, and Laura was inspired to share a family secret.

"You know," she started, "I can understand what Mrs. Comstock is going through right now. I never told you this, girls, but perhaps this story will help you. Before you two were born, I had a baby boy who died.

It was an unexpected death just like this one. He had typhoid. I didn't think I'd ever get over his death, but I knew I had to be brave. Mrs. Comstock will eventually get there. She just needs time."

"Oh!" said Nelle. "So, I'm not the firstborn!" She thought a few minutes, her eyes wide with shock. "So, my baby brother is buried somewhere back at Schell City? He's in the ground just like Jude is going to be in a few minutes?"

"Yes," assured Laura. "That's what has to happen. You just have to get used to it."

Eventually the group arrived at the cemetery and found the grieving family. No one was talking. Along the eastern ridge at the back of the cemetery, stood seven somber old pines. Their height cast a shadow over the small crowd. Laura cautioned the children to stand back out of the way. The pastor was reading the Bible over an open grave. As Laura moved to the side of the mother, Nelle and Hazel wandered away to another grave and discovered a wooden tombstone that seemed to tell a story.

Hazel spoke first. "Look at this sad little marker. 'Baby Charles. Asleep in the arms of Jesus' is what it says."

Nelle added, "He died in the same year he was born, and it was only two years ago. Look. 1896-1896. That's like my baby brother I just learned about."

Opal and Fred had joined them by then and had found a carving of a rosebud painted yellow at the top of the marker. "Oh, look," said Opal, "I'll bet his mother loved roses."

On the trip back home, the sun was just about to set, filling the western sky with a tangerine glow. The five travelers were very tired, the oldest reliving old grievings, and the four younger ones tired from their journey into the harsh reality of living and dying.

CHAPTER TWENTY-THREE

Concerned about the grief of Mrs. Comstock at the funeral and beyond, Laura and Jane paid her a visit two days later. On the way to the house, they planned what might help. Laura decided she would share her feelings on the death of her infant son back in Vernon County. Jane wanted to tell her that Fred said good things about Jude even though he was his desk mate for only one week.

On the door was a black ribbon wreath left over from the funeral.

After a few minutes, Sarah Comstock slowly opened the door and invited them in. Her disheveled brown hair and ashen face told so much. She thanked them for coming, but she couldn't keep from crying. Laura asked about the children's notes that they had prepared at school.

"Yes, that was a wonderful idea, but they came the very day Jude died, so he never saw them," said Sarah. "I just can't get the strength to read them yet, myself."

"Well, Sarah, why don't you let us open them and share the kind thoughts with you?" suggested Jane.

This idea seemed to please Sarah Comstock, so the reading began. About halfway through the stack of notes, Sarah Comstock walked to the window, wiped her tears with her apron and told them that was all she could stand to hear and that her heart was breaking at the warm thoughts Jude would never know.

"But think of the kind memories he left behind for his friends," said Jane.

Laura added, "I think Jude can hear these notes. I feel that he knows we are all here and those notes were not wasted."

Sarah Comstock said, "Jude was so dear to me. Please forgive my sadness. You both have been very thoughtful throughout this awful time, but Jude was my only reason for living. I am struggling each day to find any reason to go on."

This chilling thought caused Laura to say, "Then please let us keep coming to visit. We want you to know that we care about you."

Just then Mr. Comstock came in from the cornfield and thanked Laura and Jane for their visit. He left again to go outside and draw water for the kitchen chores.

"That's the signal that I need to start dinner preparations. I'd better get busy. Thanks for coming." With an expressionless face and reddened eyes, she saw them to the door.

Walking back home, the two friends were planning ways to bring any cheer possible to that grieving household. Then they tried to understand why they weren't allowed to share the rest of the children's notes with the mother.

"Well, maybe she is so deep in despair that she can't bear to think of the friendships Jude is missing and will never know," suggested Laura.

"What about having a few of the schoolmates come for a visit?"

"That's a great idea, but I feel she is not ready yet," cautioned Laura.

The very next day Laura and Jane returned to the Comstock cabin, hoping to have an easier visit. They were surprised when Mr. Comstock met them at the door.

"You've come at a bad time, ladies. Sarah is missing. I've spent the day trying to find her. Some days she has spent hours at Jude's graveside talking to him, but she isn't there. I've searched all over that area. Last night after dinner she just disappeared. I've been to all the nearby homes and alerted them. I just started out to go into town and see what Sheriff Scoggins can do."

"Oh," said Jane, "You need someone to go with you. Let us get Anderson or Frank to help."

"No. I'm determined to set out right now. I've wasted enough time just thinking I should be here when she returns."

"Then let me stay here to watch for her," insisted Laura. "You're right. She'll probably return here, and she'll worry if the house is empty."

"That's a good plan. I must leave now," said the weary farmer as he started his long walk to the sheriff's office.

For the next week, the whole town of Pawnee and the neighboring countryside knew the story of the missing woman. One anonymous donor had even set up a reward of $100.00 just in case someone had kidnapped her. A family that lived near the cemetery checked daily for her appearance at the gravesite. Various churches set up prayer vigils. The Baptist church provided food for Mr. Comstock.

Early Saturday morning, two boys, Sam Clayton and Shelby Frick, went fishing at Black Bear Creek. They had worked up quite an appetite and had taken a break from their work to find their lunch. When Sam walked to the scrub oak where he had left the picnic basket, he saw something that didn't look quite right. As he drew nearer, he saw the upper half of a body that had washed up after the previous night's storm.

"Shelby, come here!" he screamed.

By the time Shelby had put down his fishing pole and run to help his friend, Sam had identified the face.

"Yuck. Don't look, but I think it's Jude's mom!" cried Sam.

"I'm gonna get sick!" sputtered Shelby.

"No time for that. I'm gonna start running and you'd better follow."

The two took off as fast as they could. They were too scared and sick to talk, but both knew they should tell the sheriff. Within ten minutes two frightened boys arrived at the town square and made their way to Sheriff Scoggins' office. Entering the musty room, the boys both tried to talk at once. The bewildered sheriff said, "Calm down, boys. Shelby, you tell me first."

"We found her. Mrs. Comstock. She's down at Black Bear Creek. Dead!" blurted Shelby.

Sam added, "Yeah. She's drowned. She looks awful, but I'm pretty sure it's Jude's mom. There are black vines all over her face, but that sure looks like her!"

"Thanks, boys. You are two brave fellas, and you've helped us. Now my deputy will see that you get home all right."

Sheriff Scoggins ran next door to the shop of Bill Means, the undertaker, where he secured a horse and wagon for Sarah Comstock's trip back home. At the creek's edge, they pulled the bloated body out of the water, removed the blackened vines, determined there was no foul play and prepared themselves for meeting the bereaved husband.

"It looks like a case of accidental drowning to me," said Means.

"Well, I didn't see any wounds or signs of a struggle either, so I was thinking maybe she just gave up her life willingly," suggested Scoggins.

"Aw no, Scoggins. You don't mean suicide?"

"I don't like that word. It seems in her state of mind, with her grief over her son, she just couldn't face another day. Maybe she was temporarily crazed."

"Well, whatever you call it, we've got to notify that poor husband, and that's gonna be hard," added Means.

"You deal with grief all the time. I thought you'd be hardened to this kind of thing."

"No way. This is different with a man losing his son and then his wife just giving up this way. This is just plain rotten."

Arriving at his shop, Mr. Means arranged the body for preparation, then joined Scoggins for the sad journey.

Meanwhile, word had traveled from the two boys to their mothers and to a rural postman who shared the news with Laura and Jane on his route. After their initial shock, they tried to understand the gruesome facts.

"I think she probably walked out into the creek and let the water drink her clothes until they pulled her down. She may have been so overwhelmed with grief that she didn't realize what was happening---just like Ophelia," said Laura.

Jane asked, "Ophelia who?"

"That's in <u>Hamlet</u>, but she was driven crazy with grief, and I think Sarah Comstock was a bit unhinged at the end also. You remember how she was that last time we talked with her. If only we had been able to give her some hope," murmured Laura.

"We'll never know if she fell in or hit her head or what, but she had a burden she couldn't bear. Her final thoughts will always be a mystery. We can't blame ourselves. And remember, I didn't have your marvelous English teacher, so I don't know all those book people you love to talk about," added Jane. "But speaking of books, I'll bet the history books will praise the ruggedness of the pioneers who came out west and fought with such courage. However, they will probably leave out stories of the Sarah Comstocks who broke under the hardships of this kind of life."

CHAPTER TWENTY-FOUR

Next week the Mansfield children were gathering eggs from the chicken coop as Laura was preparing dinner. Opal and Owen were afraid of one of the hens who always chased them. Nelle led the way and let her siblings hide behind her. As Nelle kept the annoying hen busy, Opal and Owen quickly collected the eggs. While Opal was closing the chicken-wire gate, Owen noticed an Indian man and a little boy coming over the hill. Before either girl could say anything, he ran to his mother yelling, "Help! The Indians are coming!"

Laura was busy cooking a possum stew over a campfire and called to Nelle. As Nelle took over the cooking, Laura wiped her hands on her apron and waited for the visitors to arrive.

Walking slowly toward the sod house was White Eagle, holding the hand of his three-year-old son George.

Nelle watched her mother greet the two visitors, and she called her brother and sister over to the campfire. As she stirred the stew in the big black kettle, she cautioned the two children to be on their best behavior.

"Owen, don't look like you just saw a ghost. That's Mr. White Eagle, and all of us must be very nice to him. He is our friend. You can talk to that little boy of his.

He's near your age. 'The Indians' is a rude way to describe our guests. 'The white boy' would not be a kind way to talk about you."

Owen looked down at the ground in an apologetic way. "I know. I'll be better."

Opal patted his head and started to lead him out to meet the newcomers. Before they could get very far, Laura was returning with White Eagle and his son.

"Guess what!" called Laura. "We're having guests for supper. Opal, you can set two more plates."

Opal hurried to find the two pan lids that often served as plates when needed. She knew that two more at the table meant less food for each person.

As soon as Anderson returned from the field and discovered the surprise appearance of his landlord, his heart sank. He knew the reason for the visit. It was already the middle of May, and the first rent payment was due, but he was not ready. He knew he had to stall for two more weeks. Maybe Laura's good cooking would get the landlord in a pleasant enough mood to understand the problem.

He greeted White Eagle and little George, shaking hands and showing them to the outdoor table. Chairs were sawed off tree trunks, so all nine people had a seat. Lucy joined them, wagging her tail beneath the table in hopes that any dropped food would come her way.

After White Eagle returned thanks, they all prepared to dip their own portion of the stew with a gourd. Laura pointed out that the possum was caught early that morning. Everything was going well until White Eagle suggested to little George, "Dig deep and get puppies!"

The word "puppies" made Opal start sobbing. She grabbed Lucy from under her feet, and ran to the back side of the soddy. Laura nodded to Nelle, who immediately asked to be excused and walked to her sister's side. Opal was crying so hard that she couldn't talk. She was hugging the beagle as she wept.

Nelle tried to comfort her but to no avail. Opal was horrified to think anyone would eat a dog, especially a puppy, and was determined not to let Lucy be anyone's main course. Finally, Nelle made up an excuse for the comment from their guest.

"I think Mr. White Eagle really said, 'Dig deep and get possums.' You just misunderstood him. Remember, Mama had just bragged on the fresh possum."

Opal shook her head and argued, "Oh, no! 'Puppies' was what I heard!" Then she started crying all over again at the word.

"Now look. I'm sure the White Eagle family doesn't really eat puppies. That's just a phrase they use to talk about little pieces of meat. It's like people who say they were scared to death. They don't really mean they died. It's just a way to make their talk more lively. I'll bet they would really be sorry to think you were so scared by a little family saying they use."

Opal seemed to calm down a bit but was still being cautious. "I'm not so sure about that," she said. "He sounded like he wasn't kidding."

"Well," added Nelle, "I'm sure about this. You'd better pull yourself together and go back and apologize. Mr. White Eagle could kick us off this farm if we're not careful. No telling what Mama and Papa are saying to him right now."

Opal dried her tears and slowly walked back around the soddy to rejoin the family. No apology was made because the talk had already begun between the two men. They had wandered down a path to settle some important matters.

Owen and George left the table and started a game of fetch with Lucy. The beagle loved the attention and never dreamed she had been the subject of Opal's distress. Laura, Nelle and Opal cleared the table and left the men alone to talk business.

After a short walk away from the family, White Eagle introduced the subject with "Mansfield, I guess you know I need to be paid now. This is the end of your first month living here on my land. Usually I ask my tenants for earnest money at the start of their stay here, but I gave you a chance to get settled."

Kicking at the dirt in the path, Anderson grimaced, cleared his throat, and replied, "I'll be honest with you, sir. I just don't have the cash yet, but I think I can get it for you in two weeks. I'm trying to sell my good horse, but so far I haven't had much luck. And I haven't had time to bring in a crop, and the chickens haven't given us enough egg money to amount to much."

After hearing the weary and hopeless tale, White Eagle scratched his head, looked Anderson straight in the eye and said, "How much do you want for that horse?"

Anderson was shocked. "Well, Blaze is a hard worker. Belle and Blaze brought us here all the way from Missouri. His only drawback is that he fears crossing rushing water after our bad experience in the Arkansas River. They say that horses have good memories, and I guess he'll never forget that time. He stands fourteen hands high, and I really think he's worth fifty dollars. You can check his teeth, and his hooves are in good condition."

With no hesitation White Eagle said, "I trust you without giving that horse an examination. Sold. Can I ride him home?"

His head swimming at the quick sale, Anderson was overjoyed. "You bet you can ride him away. Just give me a chance to let the children say goodbye to their friend."

As Laura looked down the path at the two men returning, she was puzzled at the smiles on both their faces. Patiently she waited for an explanation. When she learned that the horse transaction resulted in two month's rent being paid, she rejoiced over the extended time period for seeing a crop or two come in for harvest. At this point, the family was breaking even. She prepared the children for the departure of their horse.

Soon Nelle, Opal, Donna, Daisy and Owen were rubbing Blaze's muzzle for the last time. Through their tears they watched an Indian man and his Indian son ride off into the sunset with the dear horse that had brought the family to Oklahoma Territory.

Seeing the sadness on their faces, Anderson said, "Just remember this. We are going to see a lot of White Eagle. Every month he'll be back for the rent, and I imagine he will be riding a horse named Blaze."

That night as he heard their prayers, Anderson was not surprised that Owen included a special God Bless for his favorite horse friend.

CHAPTER TWENTY-FIVE

Early one morning in May as the Barnes and Mansfield children were walking the two miles to Oak Grove school, Fred Barnes heard a strange noise coming from a ramshackle cabin on the left side of the path.

"Hey! Did you all hear that?"

"What? I didn't hear anything," answered Opal. "Come on. You're lagging along, and I don't want to be late."

"Well, you can just go ahead. I'm going to go over and see what's going on," said Fred.

The three girls kept on walking as Fred sneaked up to look through a window. For the past week, he had become very curious about the creepy old house which had always seemed to be deserted.

As he peered through the dirty window, he saw several broken chairs and a lot of cobwebs. Then out of nowhere he saw a white figure flying across the room and disappearing from sight. He waited and nothing made a sound. All he could imagine was that he had seen a ghost. He had heard that ghosts could disappear when necessary. With a weak feeling in his knees, he started running as fast as he could; then he saw the girls a short distance ahead. He assumed a brave attitude and tried to look sure of himself.

"So what did you see in that spooky old house?" asked Nelle. "Was it a big scary hoot owl?"

The girls laughed at the thought of Fred letting an owl almost make him late to school.

Opal asked, "Was there a ghost that chased you away?"

Fred didn't answer. He had just realized he had left his *McGuffey's Reader* back at the cabin. This was the morning to discuss the description of "Poor Davy." Maybe Miss Wheeler wouldn't notice his missing book, but he hadn't read carefully enough last night to remember all the details. This might be the day she would put him back in the First Reader.

Just then the children heard Miss Wheeler ringing the school bell as she greeted her students for another day. All morning Fred squirmed at his desk for fear the teacher would see that he was sharing his seatmate's book. Lucky for him, she was preoccupied with the school examiner who was paying a quarterly visit to check up on the school and the teacher.

At lunch break, Fred pulled Shelby Frick over to the side of the playground and made a desperate request.

"You did what?" exclaimed Shelby.

"I know it sounds crazy, but I left my book a mile back there on the way to school, and I need you to go with me. We'll get back in time. We can run."

"Well, why can't you go by yourself?"

Fred chewed on his lip and said, "It's a long story, and we're wasting time. It will be good exercise."

"O.K. I'll go, but you have to explain this crazy problem on the way," insisted Shelby.

The two boys discreetly disappeared around the side of the schoolhouse and took off running. Halfway there, Fred knew he had to tell Shelby the truth.

Stopping to get his breath, he got up his courage and said, "You know that crummy old shack by the side of the path?"

"Sure. It's the old Dewhurst place. Old man Dewhurst died in there last year. I heard he still haunts the place," added Shelby.

"No kidding? Well, you may be right because that's why I didn't want to go back there alone," admitted Fred.

"What do you mean?" cried Shelby. "I'm not going near the place if you saw something!"

"Now, I can't be real sure, but there was a white thing fluttering around in that room this morning," whispered Fred.

"Aw, it was probably an old curtain," suggested Shelby.

Then, as they came around the bend in the road, in front of them was the mysterious shack. The boys walked slowly now, trying not to step on any noisy twigs to alert the ghost. There it was. The treasured textbook lay just by the window where Fred had dropped it in his frightened state earlier in the day.

"I'll just reach over there and get it," said Fred.

"Don't look in the window. I've heard that ghosts don't like it when you see them the second time," suggested Shelby, half-joking and half-serious.

Shaking all over now, Fred closed his eyes, reached for the book and started running. Shelby was close behind. Being late or seeing a ghost. Which was worse?

By the time they reached the school door, lunchtime was over, and classes had been in session for twenty minutes. The tired, dusty boys walked sheepishly to their seats.

Miss Wheeler very calmly cleared her throat, looked at the two wayward students and told them to stay after school for an explanation. Fred and Shelby knew what was ahead. There would be a choice: they could choose ten licks with the paddle or a home visit from the teacher. Each way was a sorry end to their day. They had even missed lunch, but right then they had no appetite.

At the close of school, Nelle, Opal and Hazel sat on the front steps, trying to hear what was happening to Fred and his friend. They couldn't hear any words, but the paddle licks were very clear. How they wished they could have heard the story being told to that teacher.

They never found out what happened, but the two boys were honest about their fears.

Fred began, "Miss Wheeler, can we trust you to keep this story a secret if we tell you the truth?"

"I will respect you and thank you for your honesty," said the kind lady.

"Well, I don't know if you believe in ghosts or even if I do, but I think I saw one in that old Dewhurst cabin. It's all crumbly and looks haunted, so I went over to peek inside this morning, and I think I saw a ghost!" whispered Fred.

"Go ahead," responded the teacher, suddenly realizing that no one had ever told her of a real encounter with a ghost.

"Then here's the embarrassing part," continued Fred, trying to look her straight in the eye. "I was so scared that I dropped my book, my McGuffey's, and ran away. Later I realized my book was gone. I'm sorry, but I talked Shelby here into going back with me to get the book. It's not his fault. He was just being a good friend."

Fred felt that he was about to cry, but he bit his tongue to hold back any tears. Miss Wheeler thanked Fred for his honesty, but told him he should have been honest from the beginning. She couldn't be too harsh with Shelby who had been caught in a terrible dilemma. She couldn't stop thinking that Shelby was very brave to face such a task especially after his recent discovery of a drowned woman.

The three sisters never heard the real story even though they did their best to get Fred to tell them. However, they did notice that Fred always walked a little more quickly every morning as he came to the old Dewhurst place.

CHAPTER TWENTY-SIX

One week later, on the way to school, Fred was feeling brave as the four students walked along the path. This time he forced himself to look directly at the shack to see if anything fluttered at the window. There was nothing strange to see, so he breathed deeply and kept on walking. Then ever so faintly he heard an eerie whistling noise. It was so distant it could be mistaken for a bird. Yet, something deep inside Fred told him it was a human sound. Troubled, he quickened his pace and told the girls to hurry up.

In a few minutes, there was a rustling in the leaves that had fallen from an old hackberry tree.

"Oh, no!" cried Opal. "It's Lucy following us. Who'll take her back home?"

"It's too late for that," answered Nelle, looking at the happy dog's wagging tail. "We'll just have to take her to school and deal with the problem there."

"But Miss Wheeler won't allow us to bring our pets to school!" said Opal.

"I'll bet the kids will love to see us coming in the door with a dog," laughed Fred.

All the rest of the way Fred was so caught up in the idea of a dog at school that he almost forgot the scary whistling sound a mile back.

Beth Parsons was on the schoolhouse porch waiting to greet her friends, and she was thrilled to see the loveable dog.

"Oh, Lucy," she said. "How nice to have you join us today." Then she rubbed the dog's ears and laughed at the wagging tail.

The laughter stopped when Miss Wheeler appeared at the door to ring the starting bell.

Bewildered at the new situation, she remembered that a firm decision had to be made. Animals did not belong in a schoolroom, and a very bad precedent could not be allowed.

"Would one of you like to tell me why you brought the dog today?"

Nelle replied, "Lucy must have escaped from her fence. We are as surprised as you, but she just appeared when we were almost here. It was too late to take her back home."

Miss Wheeler thought about the two-mile distance and knew they were stuck with the dog.

"Here's what we'll do. Lucy can stay here until lunchtime. Then Fred will have to take her back home. Can you cover the four miles and be back at school by the end of the lunch hour?"

Fred agreed. A nice walk without the girls might be fun. However, as soon as he had agreed to return the dog, he remembered the eerie whistling sound, and he shivered at the thought of walking alone by the haunted cabin.

As the new arrivals entered the schoolroom, they were greeted with giggles and clapping. Immediately the clever schoolteacher snapped her fingers. That sound resulted in a stillness of surprise and respect.

"Now, boys and girls, we have a situation that could be a problem or a blessing. The result is up to you. This little beagle has wandered away from her home. She needs to find solace here for the morning. I think she is a bit frightened by all of you."

"I know you love your pets if you have them. The rule is that we don't bring our pets to our place of learning. However, we must do our work and, at the same time, provide shelter for this dear animal."

"Fred, I'll put you in charge of little Lucy. If she misbehaves or needs to go outside, you are responsible. Since your desk is near the door, you two can come and go easily."

Fred took Lucy to his desk and told her to lie down. Since his seatmate, Ben, had been absent for the past two weeks, there was extra room for the little traveler. Within five minutes, Lucy had snuggled up to Fred's feet and was snoring softly. Fred glared at Beth Parsons, who giggled at the sound. No one else dared to respond to the sweet dog noise. As Fred protected Lucy in the morning, he hoped she would protect him on the long walk home.

CHAPTER TWENTY-SEVEN

At the close of the morning lessons, Miss Wheeler took Fred and the dog outside.

"Now I want you to understand why I am sending you on this special errand, Fred. I have never sent a student home in the middle of the school day, but I think you can understand why this is important."

"I'm all right," he murmured.

"Well, I know Lucy isn't even your dog, but I can't send Opal or even Nelle back by herself. You're a brave boy, and I trust that you will get Lucy back to the Mansfield farm since you are their next-door neighbor."

"I'll come straight back, but it might take a while," he added.

"Be careful, and don't worry if you are late," said the schoolteacher as she hugged the dog. Watching the two start down the dusty path, she prayed that she was doing the right thing.

When lunchtime arrived, Fred opened his satchel and pulled out the fried egg sandwich that his mother had prepared with breakfast leftovers. Sniffing at his heels, Lucy begged for any portion that might fall her way.

"You've earned a bite," he said as he dropped a nice chunk of egg and bread on the ground. Even though she had broken two cardinal rules by escaping from her fenced home and crashing in on a school day, her excellent behavior at the foot of his school desk was worth a small portion of his lunch. Gulping water from a small jar, Fred felt better about the whole morning. He was sheltered from the noonday sun by some overhanging cottonwood trees. Their canopy lasted for a good while and made him think how sad it was for the other students to be stuck in a schoolroom.

Then it happened. The shaded path ended abruptly, and he felt the sun's rays on his face. In spite of the heat, he was shivering all over his body as he glanced to the right and saw it. The old Dewhurst place was twenty feet away. Lucy sensed his fear and started a low growling as if she had seen an enemy.

"I'm not going to be afraid," he murmured to himself. "There's no one here. I'll just prove it to myself."

He cautiously walked toward the window that had revealed the eerie billowing image and knew he had to solve the puzzle for himself. Lucy was still growling, and Fred's hands were sweating and shaky.

"Just two more steps, and I'll be looking in the window." Fred whispered in a quivering voice.

He grasped the flaky windowsill and peered through the filthy glass. A baby squirrel hopped onto a dusty table and shook its long brown tail.

"I'll bet that's what I saw. That squirrel made me think of a ghost," he said chuckling in an attempt at a brave attitude. "Well, so much for the haunted house."

Lucy was eager to leave the creepy yard with its crumbling shack, and Fred with renewed energy started walking more briskly. He even began to whistle.

The whistling came to an abrupt halt when he said, "Squirrels can't whistle!" The mystery was not solved.

Someone or something had definitely whistled from that forlorn house earlier in the day.

Gloomily, he finished the excursion to the Mansfield farm, explained Lucy's morning adventure, watched as Laura Mansfield put the dog back in a secure enclosure and started back on his two-mile return trip.

At first he thought he could just stay at home. He would be late anyway. Miss Wheeler owed him that free afternoon. Then he remembered how the school friends would pick on him for skipping school. Besides, maybe he would be looked at as some kind of hero. No one else at Oak Grove School had ever done a good deed like this one. Lucy wasn't even his dog.

His hero image took on a happier aspect. He began to walk with more assurance, and he was even looking forward to his return. Maybe if he could time his entrance for ten or fifteen minutes into the lesson, he would get more attention.

Suddenly he met up with the break in the trees. The sun's rays hit him in the face. Now on his left he saw the old Dewhurst place. In an attempt to be brave, he yelled, "You don't scare me, Mr. Squirrel." And he added a whistle solo of "Yankee Doodle."

Immediately an echo of the same whistle tune came from the dirty window. It was followed by a young voice. "Fred, come over here."

Riveted to the spot, Fred was speechless. Then he saw his schoolmate Ben Waldrup climbing out of the window.

"Ben, what are you doing in this awful old place?" asked Fred.

"Is there anyone with you?" asked Ben, searching for eavesdroppers.

"No, I'm alone. I'm just heading back to school. Why haven't you been in school this week or last week either?"

"Come over here where we can talk. I can't let anyone hear this," cautioned Ben.

He showed Fred a shadowy grove of willow trees and told him to sit down.

"I've taken on a new life. I'm not goin' back to that school."

"But, Ben, you can't just quit school. It's not such a bad place," pleaded Fred.

"Maybe not for you, but I just can't do it. You know I'm still in the Second Reader, and I was thirteen last month. I'll never get anywhere trying to do book learning. I've found a better way. You remember the old Doolin gang that hung out in the caves around Pawnee?"

"I've heard my folks talk about them. But they all got arrested, and Bill Doolin got shot," insisted Fred.

"Sure, that's the truth. But there are some holdovers that are still pulling off some good robberies. They hide out in those Pawnee caves and do a lot of horse stealing. Sometimes they do holdups on that country road that runs from here to Blackburn. They're planning another job over at Skedee, and I get to be part of that one," bragged Ben. "It's going to be a sure thing. Right now they have just one guy running the Skedee bank. That should be pretty slick, don't you think? They promised me that I wouldn't have to do any of the shooting. I'd never kill anybody. I promise."

"Oh, Ben. You've got to get away from here. Don't be a low-down crook," begged Fred.

"It's different with you, Fred. You'll probably be able to get a good job or run a fine farm. I'm just no good.

You remember how I was always picking fights at school. Besides, these guys may be renegades and crooks, but they make good money. Those stolen horses sell for a high price if you steal really good ones and know all the angles. I just wanted to say 'Hi' when I saw you this morning. That's why I whistled," Ben admitted.

Fred asked, "How can I help you?"

"Just promise me that you will never tell anybody about this. I'll be careful, but I'll be in a lot of trouble if you ever tell anybody anything I said. These guys aren't real friendly when you break the rules. So go on back to school. This old house is a rest stop for the gang sometimes. I promise not to whistle anymore. Gotta go now. Bye." Then he disappeared into the woods.

Fred wondered how anyone could be as messed up as Ben. He couldn't tell anyone, but he wanted to help. For a mile of walking he just kept groaning over the mess Ben had fallen into. Now he wished that old Dewhurst place was a haunted house. At least a ghost wouldn't risk his life every day he went to work.

CHAPTER TWENTY-EIGHT

The next day on the way to school, Fred said, "I think Miss Wheeler is a fine lady, don't you?"

Nelle agreed but asked what caused him to say that.

"Well, she is strict and not afraid to use the paddle, but she is fair. That's all," replied the boy.

"I really like her hair, the way she pulls it up in a bun and still some little curls creep out. I wish mine would do that," added Opal.

"Do you suppose she ever lets it all fall down around her shoulders?" asked Hazel. "I'll bet she'd really look special then."

Fred interrupted with "You girls missed the whole point of what I said. She treated me fairly and listened to me when I was late after lunch. I was not talking about her hair. That's girl stuff. I wish I had some guys to walk to school with every day instead of you folks."

"Well," said Opal, "she is a very pretty lady. You have to admit that. I wish we knew more about her."

Nelle asked, "Why don't we ask her to tell us about her family and where she came from?"

Opal suggested, "Yes, Nelle. You do that when we get there today. You're the brave one."

Just then the four students were opposite the Dewhurst place. Opal giggled and punched Hazel.

They watched Fred as his eyes were riveted to the right side of the path.

Hazel asked, "Fred, do you want to go visit that old Dewhurst shack?"

Fred didn't answer. He just walked faster and was soon leading the others to the schoolhouse. As they approached the front porch, they saw the lovely teacher at the door, ringing the bell and greeting the students.

Opal whispered, "O.K., Nelle. You ask her. Maybe she'll tell us her story today."

"I'm not afraid," replied the older sister, and she walked up to Miss Wheeler with her request.

The others quickly marched inside. In no time at all, the teacher began the morning routine, and the textbooks were put to good use. After an hour of desk work, Miss Wheeler told the students to put aside their slates and books. She sat on the edge of her desk and began an impromptu talk.

"Boys and girls, I have been asked by Nelle to give you some insight into my background. I feel that is a good idea since I have asked you to tell me about your lives."

"I was the youngest of fourteen children. You may not know what 'farm out' means, but I was one of five children who had to be 'farmed out.' That fact doesn't mean that my parents loved me any less. I was sent from our farm in upstate Missouri when I was three years old to live with my Uncle Bob, who was a very kind man. He also took over the rearing of the other four children, so I was not really separated from my family. After high school, he sent me to Springfield Teachers' College in Missouri for two years to get a lifetime certificate to teach. Then I heard about the need for teachers in the territories, and Oak Grove hired me. That is about all you need to know."

Several girls were teary-eyed after hearing about their teacher being "farmed out" by her parents, but they felt an even greater respect for the kind lady.

"Now that you have had a break, let's get back to work. It's time for the fifth reader students to practice their sentence diagramming," said Miss Wheeler as she erased the board with an old stocking. The younger children knew their assignments were to read in their books.

One curious little girl, Sarah Dunlap, was still puzzling over the unusual life of her teacher and sent a note to Nelle. It read, "Ask her about a boyfriend. She's old enough for one."

Before the note could reach its destination, it was read by two other girls who giggled, and then it was intercepted by a watchful teacher. Sarah's face went pale, and she bit her lip.

Suddenly as the class watched the drama unfold, Miss Wheeler laughed aloud after reading the message.

"Well, it seems I didn't complete my autobiography. An anonymous person in this very room wants to know if I have a boyfriend. And that person says I am old enough."

Two boys gasped, and the others were very still.

"I could say it is none of your business, but I don't want to be rude. I'll just tell you that when I get a boyfriend, I'll share the news with you."

She smiled with her blue eyes twinkling and proceeded to get back to the grammar lesson. Although the clever teacher had identified the handwriting in the note immediately, she never revealed that information.

Walking home that afternoon, Opal wanted to know why Miss Wheeler was sent away from her parents. She couldn't see how a mother and father could be so cruel. Nelle tried to explain that fourteen children could be a great expense and that Uncle Bob must have been able to afford to raise those five children and even pay for college. Nelle tried to paint a happy picture of the young life of their teacher and her very kind uncle.

Opal still asked, "Does she write letters to her parents?"

At this point, Fred was tired of the nosey questions. "Why don't you girls just give up all this nonsense. We know enough—maybe too much. I'm just glad she plays basketball with us at recess and can still get back to some serious teaching after lunch."

"Boys are no fun," muttered Hazel as she sighed loudly.

No one else said a word for five minutes. Then Nelle caught sight of some wild plums ahead and suggested they all find a snack. The sweet fruit brought a welcome diversion for the four weary students.

CHAPTER TWENTY-NINE

Early the next day a tall horseman was riding toward the Oak Grove schoolhouse. Across his saddle, he had placed a fresh bouquet of wild sweet peas he had found along the path. Their pungent aroma and beautiful pink blossoms reminded him of his mother's garden, but a younger woman was on his mind.

He was remembering last night at choir practice when he stayed late just to speak to her. The other Methodists had drifted away, and he had a chance to get better acquainted with the pretty soprano as he offered to walk her home. Now it seemed quite proper that he follow up with a visit to her at her workplace.

Soon the good-looking man saw the one-room schoolhouse atop a hill. Outside was a brown horse tied to a comforting shade tree. After securing his own horse nearby, he stepped up to the door and knocked softly. A surprised Miss Gertrude Wheeler opened the door to her handsome visitor.

"I hope I'm not interfering with your schoolwork, but this morning was too beautiful to waste. I just had to take a ride out here to see you," announced Jeff Fulton.

"Oh, please come in, Jeff," said the smiling teacher.

He walked quickly toward her desk and placed the flowers in an appropriate place.

"Oh, how beautiful! Sweet peas are my favorite flowers," said Miss Wheeler, as she breathed the fragrant aroma.

"I know how busy you must be at the start of the day, so I'll get on my way. I just wanted to tell you how nice it was to talk to you last night," said Jeff as he walked toward the door.

The schoolteacher was pleased to see her new friend and relieved to know that he had come at such a convenient time. She mused that in five more minutes the first student would probably arrive. She remembered the words underlined in her contract: a teacher's personal life should be kept from the students.

Seeing Jeff get on his horse, she smiled as he waved and rode away. However, she didn't see Beth Parsons walking onto the school ground. Also, she didn't know that Beth would later find a small card in the flowers. It carried her nickname, "Trudy."

At lunchtime, the news was shared among four girls.

"Guess what I saw today before you folks got here!" bragged Beth.

"A frog?" suggested Opal.

"No. I don't mean you have to guess. I mean I'm about to tell you something really fun," answered Beth.

"Oh, shucks. I was ready to add some more surprising things," laughed Nelle.

"Well, are you ready for this?" interrupted Beth.

"Sure. We're ready now," urged Hazel Barnes.

"Now, this is really good, so get ready. First of all, there was a very handsome man, tall and curly haired, who was climbing on a black horse right here at the schoolhouse door," offered Beth.

"Oh, that's nice," smiled Opal.

"Now, Opal. Don't interrupt. It just gets better," insisted Beth. "As he was getting on his horse, he waved in a special way to Miss Wheeler. She was waving back with a smile that beats any smile she ever gave us."

"I'll bet that was her brother. Did he look like her? What color was his hair?" asked Opal.

"No, that was no smile you'd give your brother," added Beth, "but hold on. There's more. You know that my desk is right in front of hers, and I saw a card by some fresh flowers on that desk. The card was addressed to Trudy. Can you believe that? We thought her name was Gertrude. Now we know what her special friends call her, and that man definitely must be a special friend."

"O.K. I guess you really found some big news," chuckled Nelle. "So what are you going to do with this news? We really can't ask her about her visitor or her flowers. I think we'd better just keep all this news as our secret."

"Yes, I remember one time Miss Wheeler said if she ever got a boyfriend, she would let us know," Beth reminded the others.

"Then we'd better just wait until she tells us," warned Hazel. "And no one must ever mention the nickname."

After lunch, it was hard for the girls to keep their minds on their schoolwork. They began to see the schoolmarm through different eyes. Suddenly she was a fairy tale princess, a bride, and a mother---anything but a purveyor of knowledge.

Beth was daydreaming of Miss Wheeler dancing with the tall, handsome man and had no idea what her teacher was saying. She was imagining the swirling pink dress and Miss Wheeler's hair pulled back by a tiara of wildflowers. Beth noticed that the wildflowers were blue and they emphasized the teacher's beautiful blue eyes.

Suddenly Miss Wheeler noticed the faraway look in the girl's eyes and wondered why she was smiling during one of the most poignant passages in all of Longfellow's poems.

"Beth, what did the poet want us to feel about Evangeline as she was being sent away from her beloved homeland and had just seen her father have a stroke on the seashore?"

A startled Beth gasped and said, "I guess he wanted us to know that she really loved her dog."

Two boys in the back row laughed out loud. Beth knew she was caught in an embarrassing moment.

"Beth, there is no dog in this scene of the story. Are you all right?" asked a puzzled Miss Wheeler.

"I'm sorry. Sometimes my mind wanders," whispered a troubled Beth.

Opal felt some of Beth's pain and said a silent prayer of thanks that she was not asked the same question. Her mind was taking a trip also.

CHAPTER THIRTY

Next Wednesday night at Methodist choir practice, Trudy Wheeler stayed behind to talk to Jeff Fulton. Putting her music away, she waited in the lobby for a private moment to ask him a troubling question.

"May I tell something to Jeff, the lawyer, and not Jeff, the tenor?"

"By all means, ma'am. Fire away," smiled the lawyer.

"I am afraid one of my students is in real trouble, but no one seems to know any of the facts. I've used all the possible methods, and the results are very disappointing," complained the teacher.

"First of all, my suggestion is that you drop the mysterious tone and give me some details. I can't help if all you provide are generalities," prompted the lawyer.

"Oh, Jeff, the boy is a thirteen-year-old. Can I tell you his name?"

"Of course. Remember that what you tell a lawyer is told in confidence. What you omit will just slow down my helping you."

"O.K. It's Ben Waldrup. He has missed school for two weeks now. Last week I visited his home. What I saw there was a very sad mother whose pitiful eyes let me know she was worried sick. She seemed afraid to talk, and the father carried on a very vague and short conversation with me. According to him, Ben was not sick; he was just away. The father gave no promise of Ben's ever returning to school. When I asked if they needed help, he just said they would handle it. Should I notify the Pawnee sheriff?"

At this point Trudy was crying and unable to continue. Jeff led her to a green wooden bench on the church porch, sat beside her, and calmly said, "You have done a wonderful job in uncovering this much information. For your own sake, now you need to rely on outside help. Here's what I would suggest."

"First of all, try to be strong. You can help more if you are in control. Second, don't let the students know of any possible trouble. Third, early tomorrow morning I will contact Sheriff Scoggins. He can be a real help in these situations. This case is serious, but I plan to stay with it. My boss, Travis Hoskins, is the best lawyer in Pawnee County, and he'll give me extra time to sort out these facts."

The two choir members walked hand in hand to Trudy's house on Cleveland Street. She felt secure knowing that her six-foot friend would do his best to help. Jeff was determined to try, but he had prior knowledge that might indicate a hopeless outcome.

Next morning the countryside around Skedee was covered with hail after a surprise rainstorm. A chill wind blew through the cracks in the front door of an abandoned house on the edge of town. Five disheveled gang members were asleep on the dirty floor as one young boy came in from gathering kindling for a morning fire. Stumbling over a pile of firewood, he awakened one of the men.

"Cut it out!" growled a gnarly man nearest the door. "Can't you even start a fire without causing such a ruckus!"

"Sorry. I must have slipped," said the boy, and he cautiously stepped toward the fireplace to prepare the breakfast.

Ben Waldrup, a boy on the verge of manhood, promised himself that he would do better. This meal was an important one for the gang. It would prepare five men for a bank holdup that would be a success. Five experienced gunmen against one bank clerk in a bank full of money. What could go wrong? Then he'd get his share, and they'd ride out of town to their hideout in the cave. The excitement made him feel he had found his place in life. Finally, he was going to be successful.

As Ben's heart beat loudly in Skedee, Jeff's spirits were low as he mulled over a letter received at the Hoskins' law office the day before. The federal marshal at Fort Smith had alerted the authorities in Pawnee County that a group of outlaws had been reported to be trying to repeat the crimes of the Doolin gang around the Pawnee County area. They were probably the ones who attacked two homesteading families and one bank. Jeff wondered if a young boy might have joined this bunch of outlaws.

CHAPTER THIRTY-ONE

Anderson rose early to see the effects of the surprise rain on his crops. His main crop, corn, was well on its way and seemed to show its thanks for the moisture. There were no signs of hail anywhere in the field. Laura's kitchen garden of tomatoes, lettuce and collard greens was shining and giving off the aroma of a tasty salad.

Meanwhile, a dozen miles northeast of Pawnee, five horses were preparing for a short trip to the bank.

"Saddle up, now, and let's get out of here!" yelled the bearded man in a checkered shirt. "You, over there, what's your name. You'll ride behind Zeke on the gray horse."

Ben learned too late that he would be part of the holdup. Carefully he scrambled to sit behind the gnarly man who had yelled at him earlier. Soon they arrived at the unpaved road in front of the First Bank of Skedee. Rain from last night's downpour had pooled in the dirt, creating muddy boots for the six new customers.

"You stay out here, kid. Watch over the horses, and be ready for a quick getaway," whispered the bearded gang leader.

Too quickly Ben heard gunfire inside the one-room bank. Through the window he saw it all. The terrified bank teller was alone, and even though he cooperated with the hoodlums, he was shot twice and left to die on the bank floor.

All five men ran out of the bank, two carrying bags of money. The gunfire had alerted the sheriff, who ran out to catch the thieves. He and his deputy tried to shoot the robbers, but no one was hit except a young boy holding the empty rope for the horses.

Chaos pervaded the dirty street as the gang escaped. Doc Scribner ran from his office next door to the bank to find the boy barely hanging on after a bullet had hit him in the chest. He and Sheriff Bates carried Ben onto the porch.

A tousled grandmother entered the bank, screamed, then ran to the door to yell, "They've killed Banker Reid!"

The doctor motioned to the sheriff to help him carry Ben into the office. Ben's moaning was growing weaker as Doc opened the frazzled woolen shirt and saw the blood oozing from the bullet that pierced Ben's heart.

"Are you going to operate?" asked Bates.

Doc Scribner carefully checked the pulse, sighed and said, "No. We're too late."

Thursday afternoon, Nelle and Opal returned home from school to find their parents working hard, weeding the corn field. Laura called to her daughters to come help and tend to their farm chores. No sooner had the girls set down their lunchpails than they saw Miss Wheeler riding her brown horse at a great speed. As she slowed to greet them, she also motioned to Laura to follow her for a private conference.

Helping Miss Wheeler dismount, Laura knew that the purpose of the visit must be bad news.

"It's about one of our students. Ben Waldrup. He's been missing from school and from his family. Oh, now I have to tell the worst. He has been shot. He is dead. It's too horrible, but he joined a gang and was part of a bank robbery at Skedee."

"No, that's not possible!" shrieked Laura.

"Listen to what has just happened," continued the teacher. "The Skedee sheriff brought Ben's body in a wagon to the Waldrup house. That's how the parents learned the horrible news. We've got to get over there immediately and let those grieving parents know we care and want to help somehow."

"I'll get Jane and we'll leave right now," offered Laura. Quickly she ran to Anderson out in the field and told the story. Then the two women rode the teacher's horse to the neighboring farm.

Jane Barnes saw them approaching and sensed a problem. As soon as she heard the tragic news, she prepared her horse for the trip to the Waldrup house. Although no one mentioned it, each woman was remembering a similar tragedy over the death of another Oak Grove student.

As they rode along, Jane asked, "How did that sheriff in Skedee know Ben's name and where he lived?"

Miss Wheeler explained how Jeff Fulton's premonition had made him notify the federal marshal about a missing thirteen-year-old Pawnee County boy. Within a few hours the news of an unidentified young boy mixed up with a gang of bank robbers reached the authorities. The Skedee sheriff was notified, and he knew what a sad trip he had to take.

When the three women approached the Waldrup farmhouse, they found neighbors in the front room trying to console Abelia Waldrup. Ben's body lay on a bed just as he had been brought from Skedee. The two neighbor women said it was time to cleanse the body and prepare it for burial. One of them took Mrs. Waldrup out on the porch and motioned for the three visitors to keep her there for a while.

Miss Wheeler put her arm around the mother and held her for a few minutes until she stopped sobbing.

"We want to help in any way we can. Ben was very precious to me at school, and I wish I could have helped him more," whispered the teacher.

"Oh, ma'am. Don't feel it was your fault. We're not blaming you. When you came to visit, I wanted to tell you everything, but his father swore me to secrecy. Ben was a good boy, but he just felt helpless with his failures at everything he tried. He was a mixed-up boy. We're so ashamed," said the mother, hiding her head in her hands.

"You must know that we all have children and we are grieving for your loss of a very special boy," said Laura. "We're ashamed that we didn't work harder to include him in our lives."

"We're not church people, but we'd like something hopeful said over him," whispered Abelia Waldrup.

"Oh, I'm sure Brother Andrews could let you use the Methodist Church. I'll get him over to see you tonight," smiled Miss Wheeler.

Adam Waldrup appeared in the doorway. "Much obliged, ma'am, but you have to hear this. No offense meant, but we need a private ceremony for our Ben. He died a bank robber. It's that simple. No one can change the facts. We just need a special time for our sorrow."

And so it was. Saturday morning a small group of black-clad mourners assembled on the familiar hill east of town. The dark green pines were more somber than ever.

Reverend Andrews spoke words of comfort and hope to the survivors of the tragedy. Miss Wheeler gave a short eulogy of Ben's hard work in the schoolroom, ending with her promise that she would try harder to help each student feel loved and encouraged. A mute eulogy came from a very troubled Fred Barnes who begged to be forgiven by Ben's departed spirit for keeping the fateful promise to Ben, which he made back at the haunted house.

CHAPTER THIRTY-TWO

Viewing his rental land for the first time, Anderson had said, "Most of this prairie has never been plowed. Until recently, the only folk who knew this place were cattle drovers who herded their stock on the way to market in Kansas." He soon saw the proof when he had tried to dig the stubborn buffalo grass. Yet, the stories of the rich bottom land and the fine agricultural area of Pawnee County had encouraged him to try harder. Since a late spring planting of corn could bring a good harvest in October, he had planted as soon as the soil was plowed. However, the best crop from his efforts so far was the large slabs of sod that aided him in building the sod house for the family.

Then came a June with very little rain. Still waiting on the fate of the broomcorn, he feared that he would barely break even. He said, "Never you mind, Laura. I've heard that winter wheat is the major cash crop in Pawnee County. We'll plant it in September, and you'll see that your man is worth keeping around." He puffed on his pipe, looking out at the stubble of the failed work and swept the sweat off his brow. So far, tenant farming, not land ownership, was the future.

The gloom that began to settle inside the sod house set Laura to thinking of an answer. She heard that some shop owners were planning ahead for their winter goods sales, so she tried to imagine what she could create at home. She had a knack for needlework that might just bring some money for food in the coming weeks. Unraveling an old sweater, outgrown by Owen, she could remake it into booties, warm headgear or potholders that others might buy. Even though her crochet hook had washed away in the Arkansas River disaster, she found another. Anderson had found some soft wood down by Black Bear Creek that proved to be perfect for carving. He carved three crochet hooks, and Nelle and Opal watched their mama long enough to learn her skill. In one week, Laura and her two older daughters created a basket full of woolen goods. Nelle and Opal made pot holders while Laura crocheted the more intricate pieces.

On the first day of July, nervous yet hopeful, Laura and Nelle rode Belle into town. The three-mile trip was pleasant as long as they rode in the shade of the scrub oak trees. The unpaved main street of Pawnee welcomed them as they approached the Mercantile Store. Nelle knew better than to ask for any horehound candy even though she knew that was to be the first sight as they entered the door. Laura tied up the loyal horse, and with a basket of winter wear on her arm, she slowly pushed open the door. After a few minutes of waiting, she bravely asked to see the owner of the store.

Mr. Struthers was talking to another man and was in no hurry to stop and talk to a little lame farm woman. He obviously was the proprietor, and his conversation was keeping him very busy.

After twenty minutes of waiting, Laura began to feel the combined pressure of fear and her weakened leg.

Noticing that her mother was about to fall, Nelle grabbed her arm and led her to a nearby chair.

"Why, look who's here!" shouted a fashionable lady customer. "I do believe you're the lady we met back at Miami at the Neosho River. And, my goodness, what has happened to you since then? You look like you have suffered something awful!"

"Yes, I am Laura Mansfield. And it is good to see you again, Millie."

"Well, I bet you folks must have met with some disaster. Was it that Neosho River crossing? You know, my husband told you folks to use the ferry and not try to take any chances on that tricky river.
We had no problems at all, and after resting up at our relative's house, the rest of the journey was most enjoyable."

Laura had forgotten the loud voice of Millie Taylor, but at least the noisy woman was causing Mr. Struthers to notice them. At last he was coming over to Laura's chair.

Turning to leave, Millie added, "You really must come out to our ranch house for a visit. We have built two more rooms and a beautiful wrap-around porch."

Rapidly approaching, Mr. Struthers greeted his favorite customer with, "Hello, Mrs. Taylor. I have your new dishes that you ordered. If you want them delivered, we can handle that."

Waving a gloved hand at Laura, Millie Taylor elegantly walked to the center of the store with the owner.

"Don't worry, Mama," said Nelle. "He won't get a chance to ignore us again." She picked up her mother's crocheted items and marched proudly behind Mrs. Taylor to be the next in line.

In five minutes the proprietor came over to Laura. "Your daughter told me you needed to see me."

Laura rose to her feet, and her hands were shaking so much that she almost dropped her basket.

"I have some things here," she mumbled.

"You'll have to speak up if you want me to hear you. I have a slight hearing problem, and I am a very busy man."

Still shaking, Mama tried again. "I crochet little items that you might be able to sell. If you would like to see them, I'd be much obliged."

The owner, dressed in a dark blue business suit and a bow tie, frowned as he considered the offer. His face did not give Laura much encouragement.

Finally, he grumbled, "I have plenty of merchandise, so I don't think I'd be interested." Then he quickly turned to walk away.

Suddenly Nelle interrupted with "I'll bet these would be just great for Christmas time. My little friends at Oak Grove School would love the red mittens!" Since her mother's shyness had almost ruined their chances, Nelle started modeling the wares. "See how well these mittens fit my hands."

After a brief examination of the quality of the stitches, the busy man said, "Well, you might have something here, but I can't promise you much. I do have to make a living, you see, and I haven't started ordering any Christmas merchandise."

His wrinkled brow was still scaring Laura as he brought out a scrap of paper. "Here's what I'll do. You just leave all your stuff here and let me see if anyone shows an interest. If your goods don't move in a week, you have to get them off my shelf. Here are my terms," he said as he handed Laura the paper with his agreement.

"Oh, thank you, Mr. Struthers. I hope you won't be disappointed," said Laura as she managed a smile, her hands cold from fear.

"Don't thank me too soon. I'm taking fifty percent, just to stay in business," he added. "Come see me next week, and we'll see if you have a winner, but I'm not making any promises." Then he turned and left them to find their way to the door.

As Laura left the Mercantile Store, Nelle heard her humming a little tune. She whispered, "Mama, I haven't heard you do that since way back in Vernon County."

"Yes, I have a good feeling about our little adventure here, and the surprise visit with Millie Taylor didn't even dampen my enthusiasm."

As the two rode back to the farm, the three miles seemed so much shorter than on the previous ride. Even Belle showed a happier mood as she clopped over the wooden bridge at Black Bear Creek.

"Do you know what a help you were in there today, Nelle? Just when I thought we didn't have a chance, you made it happen. I can hardly wait to tell your papa."

"Well, that Mr. Struthers made me mad when he told you he wasn't interested. But now we can get busy and make more stuff. I predict a run on our wares!"

Nelle was right. One week later, when they walked into the Mercantile, they were not ignored. Mr. Struthers shouted out a greeting, and even stopped talking to a customer at the counter. He walked briskly to the front of the store and offered Laura a chair.

"Hello, ladies. What about some caps now? We might be having a cold winter this year, and maybe some matching caps and mittens would sell. That friend of yours, Mrs. Taylor, was in here yesterday and she even asked about a scarf with a matching shawl. She requested a deep pink. And, oh, I almost forgot. I have some cash for you. Remember, you get fifty percent. And something else. My wife said I might have been a little unfair in our terms. So, thanks to her, here is some yarn for you to use on those matching items, just so they will match. I know it's still July, but let's try some cherry red, and how about this emerald green? Christmas will be here before you know it, and you might be running out of old garments to unravel."

Astonished with so much good news, Laura was glad she was seated. As she reached for the envelope of cash and the skeins of red and green yarn, there were tears in her eyes. "Mr. Struthers, you have made us very happy. We'll go right home and work some more."

Suddenly, the gloom of the last few weeks had turned into a feeling of hopefulness and joy. This time Laura, Nelle and maybe even Belle were humming all the way back home. That night at dinner, Laura waited until everyone was huddled around the table and Anderson had returned thanks. Then she took out the envelope with the earnings and handed it to her husband. As he counted the dollar bills, he saw that there could be food for the next three weeks. "You ladies are the ones who are saving our necks this month." Then they all got hugs for dessert.

CHAPTER THIRTY-THREE

All morning Anderson had been repairing the broken rocks on the fence row that edged his property line. Now as the sun was directly overhead, he was determined to weed the broomcorn that was the remnant of last April's planting. The fish fertilizer he had salvaged from his fishing trips at Black Bear Creek had helped the crop make a good showing. An extra warm June that had thwarted the sweet corn was a blessing to the broomcorn. Tending his crop, he tried to figure how many brooms could come from this land.

"Let's see," he mused. "At 150-350 brooms per acre I could see 3000 to 7000 brooms. If only there'd been more rain, these stalks would be ten feet high by now. They'll probably top out at eight feet."

Between the figuring and the strenuous hoeing, Anderson was tired to the bone. He knew he would sleep well and wished he could find his bed soon.

Just then he saw and heard Travis Hoskins on his black horse galloping through the cornfield, and he knew something was amiss. Pulling his stallion to an abrupt halt, the older man called to Anderson, "Climb up behind me. We've got a problem, and I need your special skill."

The farmer understood immediately that there was an urgent need for some treatment to one of the lawyer's fine animals, but he asked for a moment to warn Laura why he was dashing away at the dinner hour. In less than a minute he was back on the horse and ready for the details.

As they rode along, Anderson learned that Travis' favorite Holstein cow, Lizzie, was struggling to give birth and was having serious problems. Since the nearest veterinarian lived in Cleveland, almost twenty miles to the east, it was up to Anderson to save the life of the cow and her offspring.

Approaching the ranch, he wondered what tragedy lay ahead. So many times he had seen his father struggle for hours and end up with a dead cow and sometimes with the calf dead also. He prayed this wouldn't be a breech birth.

When the two men arrived at the barn, Anderson heard the loud moaning of the suffering cow. Examining her, he saw that this situation was what he had dreaded. The calf was in the wrong position for a proper delivery. The head should come first, but it was not where it should be. It was up to him to turn the calf. He remembered that his father had been successful in this procedure with the use of a thin cotton rope.

"It would really help if you could find me some soft rope. It has to be as thin as possible. Cotton would be the best."

The bewildered lawyer-rancher began a frantic search. All he had was a tough old rope. He returned, almost in tears.

"You'll just have to use some other method. There's nothing here that is anywhere near what you need."

Trying to keep calm, Anderson spoke softly. "Then I can try another technique that could help us. Let's not give up yet."

He felt his chances of helping this unfortunate cow were slipping away, but he needed to sound encouraging. After washing his arms and hands, he tried to talk calmly to the straining cow. Frantically, he tried to visualize how the rope plan of placing a loop around the calf's jaw could be replaced by merely getting his hand up high enough to connect with the jaw and do the turning around. So he started slowly but deliberately, trying not to be intrusive to the mother, but moving toward the jaw of the little one. Every time he made some progress, the cow would push down on the unborn calf and the intrusive arm at the same time.

"How's it going?" yelled Travis from across the stall.

"We've got a bad presentation," groaned Anderson, now finding it hard to conceal his own pain from the full day of hoeing the cornfield. He didn't get more detailed about the problem. The inside structure of the cow had the basic problem of a narrow pelvis. He felt that the chance of bringing the head around first was slim to none. After all the struggle, he feared the calf was already dead. His father had lost several breeched calves back in Virginia. Carefully he tried to move the calf so that the umbilical cord would remain intact. Without that lifeline, the calf would be dead in just a few minutes.

Then suddenly Anderson felt the warm licking of the little calf's tongue. He forced his arm farther inside the cow to push his own hand toward the jaw of the helpless animal. Pushing as hard as he dared, he grasped the mouth to try for a turn. He was successful.

How he wished he had the aid of the cotton rope. But finally the head seemed to be turning as he gently applied pressure to bring it into place. The baby cow's head was ready to leave the cow first with the little body following. Slowly he removed his forearm from the birth canal. The mother provided the rest of the work, and the new calf was born.

For about thirty seconds it lay still on the barn floor all swollen and lifeless.

"Is it dead?" asked the lawyer.

Anderson made no answer. He cleaned out the little mouth. Then as a last resort he blew into the throat and started pumping the ribs. Soon, the first sound of breathing was heard, and the two men breathed deep sighs of relief.

"The little guy will pull through now. Just let that cow feel him near her, and nature will take its course."

As Anderson was patting the new mother and whispering about the good job she had done, Travis marveled at what had just happened. He couldn't have been prouder if he had experienced the birth of his own child, which had never happened. Lizzie was his prize cow, and he knew this kind of birth could have killed both mother and baby. He promised himself that Anderson would be rewarded some day for this priceless gift.

CHAPTER THIRTY-FOUR

The next morning as Anderson struggled to return to his broomcorn crop, memories of yesterday's miracle flooded his mind and brought him a feeling of accomplishment. The joy on the face of that gray-haired lawyer was a memory he would never forget. Too many days of disillusionment on his own farm had colored his outlook, but now he felt hopeful about the future.

"I saved the lives of those two beautiful creatures, so maybe I am not such a useless guy after all," he proclaimed to the empty countryside.

"That's what I was about to say," shouted a voice from behind the bur oak tree.

"Oh, hello there, Jeff," muttered Anderson, shocked to think anyone had overheard him.

"You really saved the day for my boss with your help at the barn yesterday. Travis has been telling everyone in Pawnee the great news," smiled the young man. "Mind if I join you?" he asked as he dismounted from his fine dappled stallion.

"I'd be pleased to have some company. Laura and I have been wanting to have you over ever since we got settled here. You know you are a special person to us after your life-saving work on the Arkansas."

Just then a welcoming bark from a beagle brought Jeff to his knees as he welcomed his old friend Lucy.

"Come here, my little pal. You are worth the long ride out here," he laughed as Lucy gave him a face-licking.

Joining him under the bur oak's shade, Anderson welcomed the chance to relax a while.

"How's the broomcorn coming along? Are you planning on a good harvest?" asked the young man.

"You know what? Most of the farmers are staying away from this odd crop, so at least I won't have much competition. Laura and Nelle have been reading up on how to create brooms out of my hard work."

"Your family amazes me. It takes more than a flash flood to stop you folks," said Jeff.

"Hard work is no stranger to you from what I've heard. How are you doing on your reading for the bar examination?"

"Well," explained Jeff, "those law books in my boss's office are a great help. I guess the Travis Hoskins' bookcases are the best in town."

"Be honest now. Aren't some of those volumes pretty dull reading?" chuckled Anderson.

"I guess you could cure insomnia with a few of the wordy ones, but the Blackstone commentaries are downright fascinating. Then there is <u>Black's Law Dictionary</u>. That would be my favorite since Travis gave me my own copy."

"Then would you say you are about ready to be tested?"

Sighing a bit, Jeff admitted, "The unknown factor is that I never know what kind of lawyer will come to test me."

"You mean he could be the easy-going type or a real tough examiner?"

"No. I was referring to his field of law. If he happens to be a probate lawyer, but I've studied harder in criminal law, then I'm out of luck. Of course, if he came today and tested Travis Hoskins, he'd find a ready candidate, what with Travis' forty years of experience."

Then the conversation grew a little thin; Jeff cleared his throat and got to the point of his visit. "You may have heard that I have been seeing the schoolteacher, Miss Wheeler."

"Well, I do recall my daughters mentioning the fact that their teacher seems to have a beau. And I think someone we know saw you with Miss Wheeler at the Methodist church. But that's your own business. You know how people love to talk."

"Yes, and here's where I need your help, sir. I think this young lady is just wonderful, and I'd like to tell her so. In fact, I'd like to ask her to be my wife, but I need help."

"Well, I'll be! I'm sure you are aware that I owe you so much for saving Laura's life, but I don't see what I could do about your love life. I'd say you need to ask her yourself," stammered the farmer.

"Oh, I'll do the asking. I just remember how gallant you were when you came to my cabin and saw Laura alive after almost drowning. She seemed to be filled with love for you, too. I just want to have that beautiful feeling happen to Trudy and me."

"Lands sakes," chuckled Anderson. "I think you'll say the right thing. You are studying to be a lawyer. Don't lawyers always know just how to present a case?"

"Not really. I'd be a sorry sight if I tried to be all cut-and-dried and legal with her," said Jeff.

"O.K. Then use this two-step plan. First, let her know how beautiful and wonderful she is. That will get her attention. Then second, tell her you love her and want to spend the rest of your life with her. How could she refuse?"

Jeff rose to his feet and gave Anderson a strong handshake.

"Oh," added Anderson. "Don't finish with a handshake. Instead, let step three be a good, strong kiss."

Smiling, Jeff stated, "I think I know what I'll do after choir practice tonight. How could I go wrong with your two-step, I mean, three-step plan!"

The two men walked back to the edge of the field where the young bachelor climbed onto his horse and rode off with hope in his heart.

CHAPTER THIRTY-FIVE

All morning Laura had felt the humidity as she and her children worked in the August sun. For several hours, she had tried to make a game out of weeding the struggling corn patch.

Leaning on her crutch, she said, "Come on, Owen. You and I can pull more weeds than the others, but you have to keep working." Owen kept getting distracted by the earthworms that clung to the roots of weeds.

Laura glanced at her four daughters dragging a gunny sack through the corn stalks. Nelle and Opal had filled two sacks already with the meager addition of weeds found by Donna and Daisy.

Opal stopped to rest and sit on one of the stuffed sacks. "Why don't we have some trees out here? It would be great if we could have some shade."

Nelle reminded her that corn needs sun, not shade.

"Then, isn't it about time for lunch?"

Nelle glanced at the sun to guess the time. "I'd say we are coming up on eleven o'clock. You know Momma won't stop until noon."

Donna and Daisy had enjoyed the first twenty minutes of the game but now were intent on gathering dandelions and hunting four-leaf clovers.

Opal predicted, "We'll lose this contest if we are depending on our sisters. Look at those two."

Nelle reminded her that Mama would declare everyone a winner as she always did.

Just then a clap of thunder was heard, followed by the shrieking of five children.

"All right. We're heading back home," called Laura. "Girls, bring the sacks and hurry back. Stay away from any trees."

Before the family could make it home, the patter of large raindrops began to pelt them and their dusty weed collection. A freakish wind blew in from the west and tore a weed sack out of Opal's tiny hands.

"OK. Everyone inside. This one looks like a downpour."

Laura took a quick look for Lucy, but the dog was nowhere to be found. The mother closed the door and began to calm the children.

Daisy cried out, "This is a hot place to be. Can't we open the door, Mama?"

"Just sit still and wait. This kind of storm will bring us some cooler air real soon."

A sudden scratching at the door and a series of barks let them know that Lucy had returned. Laura ran to let in a drenched dog who shook rain all over the little home. Laughing, Laura tried to towel down the beagle, but the furry pet was too excited to be caught. Laura thought how much safer she would feel if Anderson were there with them.

By now, the sky had darkened to look more like sunset than noontime. Lightning and thunder made the family and the wet dog huddle in the midst of the one-room home. At each thunder blast, Lucy growled as if to protect the family. Water began to enter under the door.

Anderson was three miles away, building a split-rail fence for Travis Hoskins. He had left the family for a two-week spell at a time when the corn crop was growing on its own. It was good money at a time when the family could really use it. So far, Laura had handled the absence of her husband quite bravely. She knew that farmers sometimes had to go off on what were called special-skills jobs to keep the bills paid, but right now she prayed for his immediate return.

At that very moment, Anderson wished he were back with his family. The sudden storm had caught him off guard. He was far from the Hoskins' ranch house and alone with his rail-splitting chores. With no place to go for cover, he watched as lightning began to strike various spots in the fields. Not far away, in a fenced portion of the ranch land, he saw cows hurrying to find a safe haven. At each crack of lightning, they each seemed to panic and move inward toward a section of hackberry trees. Travis Hoskins had sensed the danger to his herd and had set out to drive those eight cows back toward the barn.

All eight cows settled under the protection of a large oak tree. Fearing for their lives, the old rancher headed toward the tree, trying to move them away from the danger. Suddenly a bolt of lightning struck that very spot and sent its shock waves through all eight of the cattle. As two cows fell to the ground, Travis was crushed from the weight of his beloved animals. His death was instantaneous.

Standing in the nearby field, Anderson had witnessed the whole tragedy. Fearing for his own life, he now saw the calamity that nature had brought to his fine friend.

He ran through the sodden field, unaware of any possible danger to himself in order to sort out what could be done for the rancher. Struggling through the carcasses, he found Travis' body. Trying to sense a pulse, he realized there was no hope for his wonderful friend. Walking back to the ranch house, he encountered two ranch hands who came to see about their boss.

When Anderson told the story, the workers quickly set into motion a plan for the transfer of the body to the house. It was also their job to determine the proper disposal of the eight head of cattle. Anderson knew he had to notify the next of kin. Riding Belle, he arrived quickly at the Barnes' place. Frank was checking over his crops after the deluge.

"I need to share some news that will come as a shock, my friend," he said as he dismounted and shook the water from his field hat.

"Well, let me have it," said Frank.

"Your Uncle Travis was tending the cattle during this storm, and eight of the herd were hit by lightning," Anderson said in a slow and soft manner.

"Well, it could have been worse. He has more cattle," offered Frank.

"Please let me finish. In all the commotion, he was crushed by two of the cows. He is dead, Frank."

"Did he die outright?"

"Yes. I saw the whole thing," muttered Anderson. "I was in the field just across the fence."

"No! That uncle of mine always took more risks than he should have. Why didn't he send the ranch hands out to round up the cattle or why didn't he just leave them alone in a dangerous storm like that one?"

Frank was dazed and not expecting those last questions to be answered.

"Now, Frank, I want to ride into town to tell the authorities," offered Anderson. "I guess the undertaker will be my first stop."

A puzzled look came over Frank's face. "I just need to sit down somewhere." He settled down on a tree stump and rubbed his forehead. "I guess all of this information gave me a dizzy spell."

"Let's not get in any hurry, here, friend. How about letting me get you back in the house so you and Jane can sort out all of these facts."

The two farmers walked slowly back to the Barnes' soddy where Anderson shared the sad story with Jane.

CHAPTER THIRTY-SIX

The next week drew the two pioneer families together more than ever. The Barnes children joined Laura and her five while Frank and Jane rode to the ranch, then to the undertaker, then to the law office to share the news with Jeff Fulton.

Within twenty-four hours the Methodist minister had visited the Barnes' soddy to plan the funeral, the undertaker had prepared Travis' body to lie for viewing at the ranch house, and volunteers had round the clock hours for watching over the body of the deceased in the front room surrounded by the photograph of Travis and Sadie on their wedding day. Not a detail was overlooked. The Pawnee paper carried a fitting tribute to its leading lawyer, and the columnist called him a philanthropist because of his championing of so many worthy causes.

The sanctuary was filled for the funeral service. Many even made the long trip east of town to the cemetery on the hill. After the burial as people were returning to their buggies for the trip back to town, Frank saw Jeff Fulton and his fiancée, Miss Wheeler, coming toward him. The young law clerk whispered to Frank and Anderson that both of their families needed to be present for the reading of Travis' will.

"When would you like to handle all that?" asked Frank.

"I'd just as soon do it after we leave here, if you can stand one more thing today. Your homes are not far from here, and this way you can save the trip into town and back again. I know Travis always held the reading of the wills in his office, but this particular situation calls for a different plan," said Jeff.

Frank quipped, "If we can do it out-of-doors, there will be more room. Right now, our soddies won't handle thirteen people."

So the two covered wagons and the small buggy with the lawyer and the schoolteacher journeyed west to the Barnes' soddy. All seven children gathered around Miss Wheeler as she spread a quilt out for their comfort. The adults found tree-stump chairs to prepare for the reading. Anderson and Laura felt like intruders in such a family situation, but they trusted the propriety of the instruction from Jeff Fulton. He had a special place in their lives after saving Laura back on the Arkansas River.

Just then the law clerk took his place at the front of the group and began with a short explanation.

"As you know, I have been clerking in the law office of Travis Hoskins the past two years. At this moment, I am almost ready to take my bar examination. If we could chart our lives by our hopes and dreams, I would be saying that I had passed that exam and had just hung out my shingle. But in this case, I have to tell you that I am merely Travis Hoskins' representative, and will do the best I can."

"I was present at the preparation of this will and thus have signed on the line marked 'witness.' Also, Travis

Hoskins explained to me how he wanted the terms of this will to be carried out."

Then Jeff proceeded to open a brown envelope, and he began to read.

"Know all men by these presents: I, Travis Hoskins, of Pawnee, Oklahoma Territory, being of full age, sound mind and disposing memory, do hereby make, publish and declare this to be my Last Will and Testament, hereby revoking all other and former wills and codicils by me at any time made."

Three paragraphs later, after mentioning the transfer of ownership of considerable stock to the First Methodist Church, the will centered on the two families gathered around the shade of a scrub oak tree as the sun settled slowly in the western sky.

"To my beloved nephew Frank Barnes, I leave the Hoskins family ranch and surrounding farmland."

A gasp was heard from Jane Barnes, followed by a look of bewilderment on the face of her husband. She reached out to hold his hand in an attempt to steady both of them.

Jeff continued with "To my newest neighbor and newest friend, Anderson Mansfield, I leave the forty-acre farmland which I recently purchased from John White Eagle."

Anderson stood up and asked, "How can that be? No one ever told me…. I am not even a relative. John White Eagle is my landlord. I just paid him last month. I don't understand."

Jeff interrupted with "I must ask you to hold all questions until I finish the reading of the entire will."

Anderson whispered to Laura, "This can't be. There must be some mistake."

She pulled on his sleeve to get him to sit back down, and she cautioned, "Let's not argue with good news."

After Jeff returned the will to its brown envelope, Anderson drew Frank aside. The two walked to the edge of the cornfield while the rest of their families gathered together to share an impromptu supper.

Anderson began with "I want you to know, Frank, that this news is a complete shock to me. Even though I've been working at your uncle's ranch these past two weeks, there was never any mention of his plan to give me a forty-acre plot of land. I never asked him for help. You must believe me."

Frank chuckled, "I knew you'd feel this way, but don't get any ideas about giving back the land. Uncle Travis told me what he was planning for you a while back."

"But why did he do it? I'm not even a relative."

"You just have to remember how much he felt he owed you back when you saved his favorite cow and her backward calf. He told me you should have been a veterinarian because of your great love of animals and the skills you learned from your father."

"Well, I'll be! If that doesn't beat all! Do you know what this will mean to my family?"

"I think it means you don't have to pay John White Eagle that monthly rent. You're a landowner now and can start buying lumber to build a log cabin. Good old Uncle Travis."

"But, Frank, I don't feel right about taking part of your inheritance."

"Were you listening to the will? I get the ranch and the ranch house. I'm doing okay. No hard feelings. We both have had enough time living in mud huts. We are going to live like human beings now. Uncle Travis would be so happy for both families."

So, the two farming friends shook hands and joined their families and the handsome law clerk and his lovely schoolteacher fiancée for a makeshift supper in the fading sunlight.

Made in the USA
Columbia, SC
16 January 2018